Hea

The soprano finished he
into spontaneous applaus ered her head,
graciously accepting the praise.

Right behind Marta, Nancy saw one person who wasn't clapping—Rosacrucia Alba. The young singer pulled her shoulders back, as if gearing up for a fight. She clasped her hands in front of her waist, shook her dark tresses, and stepped forward. Approaching her costar, she opened her mouth to sing.

Just then Nancy's quick eyes caught sight of a pale blur descending from the proscenium arch. It looked like a large canvas sandbag, the sort of thing used to counterweight hanging scenery. . . . And it was plummeting to the stage.

Nancy leaped to her feet, though she was too far from stage to do anything other than inturrupt Rosa's first note with a warning: *"Duck!"*

Nancy Drew Mystery Stories

#79 The Double Horror of Fenley Place
#83 The Case of the Vanishing Veil
#85 The Secret of Shady Glen
#104 The Mystery of the Jade Tiger
#108 The Secret of the Tibetan Treasure
#110 The Nutcracker Ballet Mystery
#112 Crime in the Queen's Court
#116 The Case of the Twin Teddy Bears
#117 Mystery on the Menu
#120 The Case of the Floating Crime
#123 The Clue on the Silver Screen
#125 The Teen Model Mystery
#126 The Riddle in the Rare Book
#127 The Case of the Dangerous Solution
#128 The Treasure in the Royal Tower
#129 The Baby-sitter Burglaries
#130 The Sign of the Falcon
#132 The Fox Hunt Mystery
#134 The Secret of the Forgotten Cave
#135 The Riddle of the Ruby Gazelle
#136 The Wedding Day Mystery
#137 In Search of the Black Rose
#138 The Legend of the Lost Gold
#139 The Secret of Candlelight Inn
#140 The Door-to-Door Deception
#141 The Wild Cat Crime
#142 The Case of Capital Intrigue
#143 Mystery on Maui
#144 The E-mail Mystery
#145 The Missing Horse Mystery
#146 The Ghost of the Lantern Lady
#147 The Case of the Captured Queen
#148 On the Trail of Trouble
#149 The Clue of the Gold Doubloons
#150 Mystery at Moorsea Manor
#151 The Chocolate-Covered Contest
#152 The Key in the Satin Pocket
#153 Whispers in the Fog
#154 The Legend of the Emerald Lady
#155 The Mystery in Tornado Alley
#156 The Secret in the Stars
#157 The Music Festival Mystery
#158 The Curse of the Black Cat
#159 The Secret of the Fiery Chamber
#160 The Clue on the Crystal Dove
#161 Lost in the Everglades
#162 The Case of the Lost Song
#163 The Clues Challenge
#164 The Mystery of the Mother Wolf
#165 The Crime Lab Case
#166 The Case of the Creative Crime
#167 Mystery by Moonlight
#168 The Bike Tour Mystery
#169 The Mistletoe Mystery
#170 No Strings Attached
#171 Intrigue at the Grand Opera
Nancy Drew Ghost Stories

Available from Simon & Schuster

NANCY DREW®

171

INTRIGUE AT THE GRAND OPERA

CAROLYN KEENE

Aladdin Paperbacks
New York London Toronto Sydney Singapore

First Aladdin Paperbacks edition March 2003

ALADDIN PAPERBACKS
An imprint of Simon & Schuster
Children's Publishing Division
1230 Avenue of the Americas
New York, NY 10020

Printed in the United States of America

10 9 8 7 6 5 4

Library of Congress Control Number 2002113035

ISBN 0-689-85560-5

Contents

1

The Curtain Rises

"I can't understand what they're singing," George Fayne whispered to her friend Nancy Drew, nodding toward the performers on the stage.

George's cousin, Bess Marvin, leaned over across Nancy. "That's because they're singing in Italian, silly."

"Italian?" George frowned. "But I thought this opera was by Mozart. Wasn't he German?"

Bess settled back in her seat, eager to show off her knowledge. "Austrian, actually. But back in the eighteenth century, when Mozart wrote *The Marriage of Figaro,* all operas were sung in Italian. It was the fashion of the age."

Nancy grinned. "You sure have learned a lot in just a few days, Bess. Just think, last week you were as ignorant about opera as the rest of us."

Bess smirked. "That was before I found out I was going to be *in* an opera."

George and Bess had been Nancy's best friends since they were all kids. They were as close as sisters, which was important to Nancy, an only child whose mother had died when she was three. Her father, respected River Heights attorney Carson Drew, was devoted to his daughter, of course. But in many ways Bess and George were Nancy's family.

In the orchestra pit the frazzled young director rapped his white baton on the music stand before him. "Rosa?" he called out. No answer. He whirled around. "Where is she? This is her cue!" The director's anger echoed throughout the auditorium of the River Heights Theater, bouncing off the ornate gilded plaster decorating its ceiling, balconies, and the proscenium framing the stage.

"Yeesh!" George muttered, shrinking down into her red-plush seat. "Remember not to make that guy angry, Bess."

"Steven Reynolds?" Bess asked, nodding toward the director. "Oh, he's okay, really. He's just under a lot of pressure. The company has to do six shows in River Heights—three different operas, two performances each. Every opera lover in town has been looking forward to this for months. It's not often that the world-famous American Grand Opera comes here."

"I still can't believe they hired you, Bess," George

said, as the rehearsing singers, dressed in ordinary jeans and sweats, milled around the front of the stage. "No offense, but when Mrs. Nissen called to suggest you should audition, I thought she was kidding. She taught you in high school chorus class—she should know you're not *that* great a singer."

Bess pretended to pout, though she was used to her cousin George's teasing. "Shows what you know. I have a lovely coloratura soprano." Then she giggled. "Besides, Mr. Reynolds said they needed a blonde who could fit into the costumes."

"Now I get it," Nancy said. "It's all about the clothes, isn't it, Bess?"

Bess nodded enthusiastically. "I've got the most darling peasant dress for this opera—peach-colored with pink roses—and for *Aida,* which is set in Egypt, I wear a white sheath with loads of fake jewelry."

"And in *Tosca,* you're a nun," George reminded her. "In a black habit buttoned up to your chin."

Bess smiled. "With a beautiful starched white headdress. It's *divine*!"

At that moment, the singer the director had been waiting for—a slim young woman with long raven-black hair and huge dark eyes—strolled languidly onto the stage. Reynolds could hardly contain his anger. "Rosacrucia! You've played this part two dozen times already. How could you miss your entrance?"

Rosa gazed at him from underneath thick dark lashes. "Steven, *mio caro,* you know how I am with directions," she purred in a thick accent. "Every new theater, I always get hopelessly lost." She leaned over to cup a hand under his chin. "You will forgive me, won't you?"

Reynolds blew out a long breath. "Well, now that Signora Alba has bothered to join us"—he tapped his baton on the music stand—"let's take it from the last three bars of your song, Marcel."

The stocky baritone playing the title role—Figaro, servant to Count Almaviva—launched into the end of his opening aria. Nancy relaxed in her seat and closed her eyes, letting his rich voice wash over her. Though she didn't usually listen to opera music, Figaro's aria seemed familiar. Maybe she'd only heard it once before, but it was the sort of song that was unforgettable.

Nancy opened her eyes as the baritone reached the final measures of his aria. She then saw the beautiful soprano sashay next to him and curl her arms around his neck. Her full lips parted and her voice poured out—high, clear, and full of passion. Nancy felt a shiver run up her spine.

"Who's the soprano?" she whispered to Bess.

"Rosacrucia Alba," Bess said. "She's from Slovenia. She just joined the company last year. Apparently Rosa's taken the opera world by storm."

Nancy nodded. "She has a gorgeous voice."

"Not only that," Bess said, "but she's so pretty—and so young—that she's constantly in demand for ingenue roles."

"Ingenue?" George asked.

"Young girl parts," Bess explained. "Like in this opera, she plays Susanna, the maid who's engaged to marry Figaro."

Nancy thought a moment. "But, Bess, I thought looking young and pretty didn't matter so much in opera. A lot of opera singers are . . . well, hefty, aren't they? Look at that Italian tenor, Luciano Pavarotti—he's pretty big. And he still plays young lover parts."

"Having a great voice is the most important requirement," Bess said. "Singers don't go crazy trying to be skinny, like movie stars do. But if you've got a great voice *and* you look the part, you've got an advantage."

"Thank you, Rosa," Reynolds called out. Her voice broke off in midtrill, and the handful of musicians in the orchestra pit lowered their instruments. "I know you know the music. No use straining your voice," he explained. "Let's just walk through the rest of this scene and adapt to this space." He peered uneasily up at the River Heights Theater's curlicued proscenium arch. "This stage is much smaller than the ones we usually play on. I only hope the sets will fit."

"They'll fit, they'll fit," barked a middle-aged man

in grubby work clothes. He was standing at the right-hand edge of the stage, sticking a hammer in his back pocket. "We'll make 'em fit."

"Have you figured out how to use this antique scenery-changing equipment, Mike?" Reynolds called out to the stagehand.

"Piece of cake, Steve," the stagehand called back. "I've seen this stuff before. It may be old, but it works." He clomped back into the wings.

Reynolds talked the cast through the rest of the first act. A bewildering number of characters made countless entrances and exits. "I can't keep all this straight," George muttered to Bess. "Who's matched up with whom?"

"Everybody's matched up with at least two other characters," Bess said. "Figaro is engaged to Susanna, but the count is interested in her too, and so is the pageboy, Cherubino."

George squinted. "Which one is he?"

"That brown-haired woman in the black T-shirt," Bess said. "Cherubino is always played by a woman. It's what they call a 'trouser role'; it's written for a soprano voice, so a woman has to put on trousers to play it."

George shook her head. "No wonder I'm confused."

Bess laughed quietly. "Don't worry, I still get all these characters mixed up, and I've read the story outline ten times." She pointed to someone onstage. "That older woman, Marcellina, wants to marry Figaro; the guy she's plotting with wants revenge on the count for marrying the countess. Cherubino has a major crush on the countess, too, but Cherubino has a crush on every woman he sees."

"Which one is the countess?" Nancy asked, scanning the people onstage.

"She's not in this act," Bess explained. "You'll see her in a few minutes. She's played by Marta Willentz."

Both Nancy and George sat up, impressed. "Marta Willentz?" Nancy echoed. "*The* Marta Willentz?"

"Even I've heard of Marta Willentz," George said. "She sang the national anthem at the World Series last year. She's amazing."

"And she performed at the White House last year. They showed it on TV," Nancy recalled.

Bess tossed her head. "Well, once you start singing at the White House and the World Series, it's a sure sign your career is over. Willentz is nearly fifty years old now. Her voice isn't what it used to be." Spotting a look of doubt on Nancy's face, Bess quickly added, "At least, that's what opera buffs say. Rosacrucia Alba, on the other hand—everybody wants to hear her."

"All right, people." Reynolds called for his cast's

attention. "That takes care of Act One. Let's move on to Act Two. Is Marta—"

"Here, Steven," a throaty voice rang out from the back of the auditorium. Nancy pivoted in her seat. No matter what Bess said, she was eager to catch sight of the great Marta Willentz.

She came striding at a stately pace down the aisle, her chin held regally high. Marta was tall, with a pile of frosted hair making her look even taller. Her shoulders were broad, her posture erect. Nancy caught her breath. The famous soprano had the commanding presence of a queen.

Willentz emerged from the shadows into the glare of the light by the stage. "Darling!" Reynolds greeted her. He sprang off his podium and held out a hand to guide her up the temporary steps onto the stage. "If you don't mind—"

"How could I mind a rehearsal?" the diva chided him gently. "This is what we do. Perfection is our goal, but we cannot reach it without hard work. Discipline."

As she brushed past Rosa, Marta Willentz dropped a cool glance over her shoulder. Nancy saw Rosa glare back at her costar.

"Ouch," George whispered. "I guess that puts Rosa in her place for being late."

"There's no love lost between those two, that's for sure," Nancy murmured.

"I've noticed that already," Bess added. "In this

opera, they're supposed to be jealous of each other—but from what I see, they're not acting."

Marta pivoted grandly as she reached her place onstage. "Act Two, Scene Two," she enunciated in rounded tones. "Shall I begin?"

And without waiting for the musicians to strike up, Marta began to sing. Nancy felt another spinal shiver. It wasn't just that Marta's voice was strong and clear, although it was. There was something more to it—vibration, emotion, and almost some color. Nancy couldn't describe it.

The soprano finished her aria and the room burst into spontaneous applause. Marta lowered her head, graciously accepting the praise.

Right behind Marta, Nancy saw one person who wasn't clapping—Rosacrucia Alba. The young singer pulled her shoulders back, as if gearing up for a fight. She clasped her hands in front of her waist, shook her dark tresses, and stepped forward. Approaching her costar, she opened her mouth to sing.

Just then Nancy's quick eyes caught sight of a pale blur descending from the proscenium arch. It looked like a large canvas sandbag: the sort of thing used to counterweight hanging scenery. . . . And it was plummeting to the stage.

Nancy leaped to her feet, though she was too far from stage to do anything other than interrupt Rosa's first note with a warning: *"Duck!"*

2

Duelling Divas

Everyone onstage heeded Nancy's warning and ducked. The heavy sandbag fell right where Rosa and Marta had been standing, and landed on the stage with a thud.

Nancy had already vaulted over the open seats in front of her and scooted to the aisle. As she raced toward the stage, cast members crowded around the two sopranos. Nancy could see that both of them were shaking from their close call.

Nancy took the steps to the stage in two strides and elbowed her way into the buzzing cluster of singers. A handsome singer had just run in from the wings to comfort Marta. On the other side of the sandbag, Rosa stood alone. Her arms were wrapped around her waist.

The sandbag lay on the floor, and sand trickled out of a split seam. Nancy glanced upward toward the rickety steel catwalk that stretched over the stage. Several similar sandbags hung from ropes near the ceiling. On the catwalk stagehands were gathered in an angry knot, gesticulating and arguing.

Reassured that the singers were safe and unhurt, Nancy ran over to a spiral set of stairs in a back corner of the wings. Pounding up the steps, she soon reached the catwalk.

"What was it doing lying loose on the catwalk?" demanded a man with a clipboard and headphones—the stage manager, Nancy guessed.

A female stagehand, about twenty years old, cringed under the stage manager's fierce gaze. "I-I don't know," she stammered. "I didn't leave it there."

"Well, who did?" the stage manager demanded. "Those bags should only be used to stabilize a flying set piece. If it's not attached to a rope, it shouldn't be lying around anywhere. Certainly not up here."

The stagehand Nancy had seen before—Mike, the director had called him—leaned on the catwalk railing. "Cut the kid some slack, Doug," he said softly. "She's new. She's probably never seen a sandbag in her life. Most theaters have switched to automatic pulleys."

The young stagehand's large gray eyes were swimming with tears. Nancy felt sorry for her. It was hard for a young woman to hold her own in a male-dominated trade. Nancy knew this all too well. Working as an amateur detective, she'd run into plenty of sexist guys like the stage manager. *They could drive a girl to tears,* Nancy thought, *and then make fun of her for crying.*

The young woman raised her chin and met the stage manager's eyes. With her short sandy hair and thin freckled face, she looked like a defiant boy. "I'm sorry, Doug. I saw the bag lying there, but I didn't think. I was too busy trying to hang this side fly. I'll know better next time. But I swear, I had nothing to do with it falling."

The other members of the stage crew dropped their eyes and shuffled their feet awkwardly, mumbling things like, "Me neither, Doug" or "I was down on the floor when it happened."

The stage manager scratched his neck. "Well, what's done is done," he said. "Luckily no one got hurt. But let's be more careful from now on." With murmurs of agreement, the crew disbanded.

Nancy sidled to the end of the catwalk, waiting for the young stagehand. "Accidents *do* happen," Nancy said as the girl passed.

Startled, the young woman stopped to stare at Nancy. "I didn't touch that sandbag!" she protested again.

Nancy smiled. "Of course not. I'm Nancy Drew,

by the way. I've got a friend who's an extra. We were watching the stage when the bag fell."

The girl shyly shook Nancy's hand. "Jackie Ahern."

"You didn't happen to see anybody else moving up here before the accident, did you?" Nancy asked.

Jackie shook her head. "No. But I admit, I don't really know the rest of the crew, and I'm not really tuned in to knowing where and when everyone should be just yet. I was hired as a temp, filling in for one of the regular hands. He got hurt last week—some kind of scenery collapse."

Nancy raised her eyebrows. "Another accident?"

Mike, the older stagehand, came up behind Jackie. "Yeah, this tour has been lousy with accidents so far. And it's almost always something to do with those two hoity-toity divas." He jerked a thumb toward the stage, where Alba and Willentz were rehearsing again.

Jackie Ahern stared down at them, narrowing her eyes. "Yeah, the big stars," she said with a tinge of sarcasm. "Well, come on, Mike, let's finish hanging that fly. Nice to meet you, Mandy."

"Nancy," Nancy corrected Jackie, but the stagehands were already back out on the catwalk.

Nancy brooded as she descended the spiral stairs. She'd been involved in enough mysteries to know when something didn't smell right. And a rash of suspicious incidents on a road tour with two major stars—that *definitely* didn't smell right to her.

At the base of the stairs she found the director, Steven Reynolds. He was waiting for her. Nancy looked apologetic. "I'm sorry—I shouldn't have gone up there without permission," she said. "I'm sure you don't need members of the public poking around. Please don't blame my friend Bess Marvin. She said we could watch if we didn't interfere—"

"I've already spoken to Miss Marvin," Steven Reynolds said crisply. "And Miss Fayne. They think you may be able to help us."

Nancy shifted uneasily. "Help?"

He glanced furtively over his shoulder and lowered his voice. "They tell me that you are an accomplished detective."

"Amateur," Nancy corrected him reluctantly. She didn't like people to know what she did.

"All the better." Reynolds pushed his horn-rimmed glasses up his nose. He reminded Nancy of a college professor, with his glasses, unruly thatch of brown hair, and pale skin. "I don't want professionals nosing around. It might create bad publicity. But you," he said, sweeping a glance up and down, taking in Nancy's jeans and red-blond hair, "you could pass among the company unobtrusively. No one must know there is a detective nosing around. This is a very delicate matter. Any whiff of scandal could ruin this tour."

Nancy hesitated. "Someone's bound to wonder who I am."

Reynolds took Nancy by the arm and led her toward a side door. "Then we'll say you're another supernumerary," he murmured as they strolled into a narrow hall. "That means you're an extra. Just like Miss Marvin. You can mingle with the cast and crew, have access to the dressing rooms, costume area, and scenery shop." He gestured at these backstage areas as they passed them. "You can climb up and down the catwalk all you like, and no one will pay you any attention. No one ever does notice the extras. They're like human furniture."

Nancy smothered a smile, wondering how Bess would feel to hear herself described as "human furniture."

Mr. Reynolds pushed open a gray metal door and led Nancy into his temporary office: a small room with a simple desk laden with phones, a laptop computer, and stacks of files. He lifted some bundles of sheet music off a metal folding chair so Nancy could sit.

"Now, for your schedule," Reynolds breezed on, ignoring the fact that Nancy hadn't yet agreed to help. "This afternoon and evening, we run through each of our three operas." He ticked them off on his fingers. "Tomorrow—Wednesday—there's a matinee of *Aida* and an evening performance of *Tosca*. On

Thursday we do *Figaro* at night. Saturday, we have a *Tosca* matinee and an evening performance of *Aida.* We wrap things up on Sunday with another evening of *Figaro.* The schedule is spread out so the principal singers can rest their voices between performances."

He fidgeted and looked concerned. "I'm afraid that both our sopranos are taking on heavy loads. Marta stars in *Tosca,* Rosa in *Aida,* and, as you know from watching the rehearsal, they both appear in *Figaro.* If anything happens to either of them . . ." He winced.

Nancy tilted her head, curious. "They don't seem to be very friendly colleagues."

Reynolds rolled his eyes. "What can I say? They are both true divas. The word was invented to refer to opera stars, you know. They get pampered and flattered and treated like royalty. They throw tantrums over the tiniest things." He smiled, pushing up his glasses again. "As director of the road company, the biggest part of my job is baby-sitting the divas."

Nancy smiled back. "But Willentz and Alba—their rivalry is extra fierce, isn't it?"

Reynolds shrugged. "Marta Willentz has earned her place in opera history. Some critics say her powers are failing, but I believe her voice is still in splendid shape for a woman nearly fifty. What's more, her musical knowledge is"—he kissed his fingertips—"superb."

"Rosa?" He went on. "She has vocal strength and a brilliant tonal quality, no doubt about it. But her musical readings are often superficial. She received shoddy training early in her career, when she was a nobody, and she learned some bad vocal tricks. That could harm her voice in the long run. Someday, yes, she could be a great star—but that day has not yet arrived. The trouble is, she thinks it has."

Nancy took all this in. "The stagehands said there have been several incidents so far."

Reynolds grimaced. "A scenery flat toppled last week. It almost fell on Rosa. Luckily a stagehand was hurt instead." He blinked. "Not lucky for him, of course."

"Of course," Nancy agreed, smirking.

"Then Marta reported a few things missing from her dressing room," the director continued. "Nothing of great value, but she was tremendously upset by it."

"Both of the sopranos have been victims, then," Nancy summed up.

Reynolds nodded. "So we can rule them both out as the culprit."

"Don't jump to conclusions," Nancy advised him. "Perhaps they are both guilty. They could be waging war against each other."

He pursed his lips. "But both were onstage today when that sandbag fell. Doesn't that prove neither of them did it?"

"Not if one has an outside accomplice," Nancy suggested.

Just then the door to Reynolds's office burst open. Nancy, startled, jumped in her chair.

She recognized the young man who barged in as the same man who had comforted Marta onstage after the sandbag fell. He was tall, with handsome, craggy features and wavy brown hair. He tossed his head melodramatically and posed with his hand on the doorknob.

"Sean, what is it?" Steven Reynolds asked, getting up from his chair. "Miss Drew, may I present our premier baritone, Sean Torrance. He sings Count Almaviva in *Figaro* and—"

His dark eyes blazing with anger, Torrance interrupted the director. "The rehearsal is a complete shambles, Steven," he announced. "Marta stalked off stage. It's serious this time, Maestro. She says she'll never again appear on the same stage with Rosacrucia Alba—and I do think she means it."

3

The Plot Thickens

All of the blood seemed to drain out of Reynolds's face. "Marta said *what?*"

Torrance cast his eyes sorrowfully to the floor. "She will never again appear onstage alongside Rosacrucia Alba."

"But they're doing *Figaro* together!" Reynolds spluttered. "They insisted! Rosa begged to play Susanna, and then Marta screamed that Rosa was trying to show her up, and she demanded I let her be in *Figaro* too!"

Sean shook his head. "I know, I was there that day. I heard everything."

Reynolds was out of his chair now, pacing around the tiny office. "The board of directors were furious. How could I let both singers sing double roles on this tour, they said. I fought to get those women what they wanted. And now this! They will ruin me!" With a huge groan, he ran out of the office to soothe his temperamental star.

Torrance sank onto the office's other folding chair. He cradled his head in his hands. "It's all my fault," he moaned.

Nancy felt confused. "Your fault? Those two were already mad at each other."

Torrance wasn't listening. "After all Marta has done for me. When I was young, who helped me find the right teachers? Marta. Who persuaded directors to let me audition for my first roles? Marta. She's been my guiding light, my mentor, for years. How could I betray her like this?"

How had he betrayed Marta? Nancy stiffened in her chair.

Sean arched backward, flinging his arms outward in an extravagant gesture of remorse. "And all for what? For the attention of that little minx—that black-haired, black-hearted Slovenian temptress. When she cast her eyes my way, I should have known better. For a mere dinner date, I broke the heart of the only woman who believes in me."

Nancy raised an eyebrow. "All this ruckus is because you went out to dinner with Rosa?"

Sean Torrance swiveled in his chair and looked at Nancy for the first time. "Hell hath no fury like a woman scorned," he said gravely.

"I'm not one hundred percent clear on this," Nancy said slowly. "Are you and Marta involved?"

The baritone looked offended. "Not the way you mean 'involved.' Nothing vulgar like that. Marta and I are artistic soul mates. That is too precious to be tainted with physical love. Rosa, on the other hand—she's a common vamp."

"So she flirted with you, and you fell for it," Nancy said, shrugging. "You're only human."

"But don't you see? The only reason she went after me was to hurt Marta," Sean insisted. "She wasn't interested in *me* at all. What a vain fool I was to fall for it!"

Nancy hid a smile. "Don't be so hard on yourself. You're a good-looking guy. Maybe she really was interested in you."

Sean rolled his eyes. "Yeah, right."

At that moment, Bess ran into Reynolds's office. "Nancy, I just heard the news! It'll be so fun to have you in the chorus."

Nancy twisted her mouth to one side. "I haven't told Reynolds I'd do it yet—"

"Of course you'll do it," Bess declared. "It's too good an opportunity to pass up! Come on, let's go get your costumes fitted."

Nancy excused herself and left Sean Torrance to berate himself. As they went through the hall Bess tucked her arm in Nancy's. "Lucky for Reynolds he found a detective who can fit into the dresses they have on hand," she joked. "Now we'll go meet Lauren Sweet. She's the costumer. She's so cool."

Lauren Sweet was a petite woman with tousled white-blond hair and overdone eye makeup. Nancy immediately liked Lauren's matter-of-fact grin. "Welcome to the company," Lauren said. "Or maybe I should say welcome to the loony bin! This place is full of wackos. But I love it."

"Nancy needs outfits for all three operas," Bess told Lauren. "Pretty ones, please."

"They're all pretty," Lauren said. "*Figaro* peasant dress, coming right up." She pulled a flouncy pale-yellow organza skirt off the rack. "Pair this with a white cotton blouse, and this." She whisked out a short green satin jacket, embroidered with gold silk roses. "You like?"

Nancy's eyes sparkled. "I like very much!"

Nancy ducked between the rolling racks and was slipping the jacket over her T-shirt when she heard the rapid *tack-tack-tack* of high-heeled shoes approaching. The rack of gowns rustled as someone brushed along them on the other side. "Lauren, you angel," purred a voice that could only belong to Rosa Alba. "Have you got a minute?"

Nancy heard Lauren answer, "Well, actually Miss Alba, I was helping this girl—"

"I'll be quick," Rosa wheedled. "It's my *Figaro* costume for Act Three. It simply won't do."

Tugging her jacket into place, Nancy stepped out. "Ready to check the fit?" she asked Lauren.

Rosa cast her a withering glance. "You, later," she said with a rude wave of her hand. "Now, Lauren, the problem is here." She pirouetted to display the rose-colored velvet bodice she wore over a thin slip. "It must be taken in. With my small waist . . ."

Nancy saw Lauren's eyes tighten. "We've been over this before, Miss Alba. The fit is perfect."

"But it's so important to the character," Rosa pressed her case. "Susanna, she is young and slim—a breath of spring. Countess Almaviva is dumpy and middle-aged. The contrast between the two must be clear, especially in the third act."

Lauren shook her head. "Your waist may be small, honey, but you need room to breathe. You have to breathe in order to sing, don't you?"

Rosa's gaze hardened, but her voice was still sweet as honey. "I have no trouble breathing in this costume, I promise. But when I stand onstage opposite the countess—the count's former love—the audience must see the difference between my figure and her . . . hmm . . . more stately build."

"You're saying Marta is overweight?" Lauren asked.

Rosa giggled. "Is right word? My English is not

perfect. But you know what I mean. Marta Willentz is a woman of a certain age. She is no chicken of spring anymore."

Lauren cleared her throat as if delivering a warning. "I already gave you a bone corset to suck in your stomach," she said tersely. "You try tightening that further—if you can." With that, she turned her back on the famous soprano and began adjusting Nancy's jacket.

Over Lauren's shoulder, Nancy could see the shock on Rosa's face. She stood still for a moment, mouth open. Then she whirled around and stalked away. The high heels of her boots clicked sharply as she went down the hallway.

Bess whistled. "Wow, Lauren, that took guts," she said. "I'll bet people don't talk to her like that very often."

Lauren waved a hand in the air. "You'd be surprised. She's a well-known pain in the neck. Turn, Nancy, so I can check the back seams"

As Nancy turned, she said softly to Bess, "Rosa sure seems eager to hurt Marta. I heard she even tried to steal Sean Torrance away from her—you know, the guy who plays the count."

Overhearing Nancy, Lauren smiled. "You mean that dumb love triangle?"

Nancy looked guilty. "I guess I shouldn't be repeating gossip. . . ."

"It's no secret," Lauren declared. "In an opera

company, we all know everybody else's business. The Rosa versus Marta thing has been like a soap opera in itself for weeks. Funny thing is, it's exactly the same story as *The Marriage of Figaro.* Older woman becomes jealous of younger woman, who may be stealing her husband away."

Bess looked thrilled. "Sean Torrance is Marta's husband?"

"Oh, no. Sean's just her protégé," Lauren explained. "But they've been close for years. And everybody knows Rosa is only flirting with Sean to hurt Marta. It's too bad. Sean doesn't deserve to be hurt. He's a good guy."

"Sean Torrance, a good guy?" a sarcastic voice broke in from behind them.

Nancy whipped her head around to see a tall woman with short, black frizzy hair leaning against a side wall. Her head-to-toe black outfit only emphasized her extreme thinness.

"Hey, Nora, what cave did you crawl out of?" Lauren teased the newcomer. "Girls, meet Nora Stubbs. She thinks she's the next Mozart."

"Better than Mozart," Nora shot back. "When the public finally hears my new opera—"

"*If* the public ever hears your new opera," Lauren corrected her. "Has Steven okayed it yet?"

"Not yet, but he will," Nora said, idly plucking an Egyptian headdress from the *Aïda* rack.

Lauren pulled the green jacket off Nancy. "This needs a few tucks. I left my scissors upstairs. I'll be back in a minute."

As Lauren skipped away Nancy seized the opportunity to talk to Nora Stubbs. "So why isn't Sean Torrance a good guy?" she asked the composer, trying to sound casual.

Nora shrugged. "He's a two-faced liar, that's all." She began to stroll toward the heavy metal stage door.

Nancy followed her. "How so?" she asked.

"Well, when I was first developing my opera," Nora explained, "he acted like my number one fan. It's about Eleanor Roosevelt. I wrote the lead role for Marta. It's certain to revive her career. Sean promised he'd help persuade Steven to produce it."

"And he didn't?"

Nora's smile twisted. "Sure, at first—when he thought Franklin Roosevelt was a baritone part. He figured he would definitely get the role. He was plenty helpful with Steven then."

Nora pushed open the stage door, and Nancy was blinded with a sudden flood of sunshine. As her eyes adjusted to the outside light she almost ran into a young man with a brown goatee and a lumpy mustard-yellow sweater.

Nora chattered on. "But then I changed Roosevelt

from a baritone role to a tenor part, and Sean totally changed his tune—excuse the pun."

"Typical opera snobbery!" the man in the sweater said. He sounded eager to pick a fight. "You composers are so prejudiced against baritones. Why should the lead roles always be tenors?"

Nora Stubbs's reaction startled Nancy. She whirled to face the man, fists clenched at her sides. "Donald Tompkins! Are you still hanging around?" She practically spit the words at him. "Don't you have anything better to do with your time other than stalk Marta?"

4

Rehearsing Revenge

Nancy felt her blood run cold. Celebrity stalkers had been known to turn deadly. Had this guy been inside the theater half an hour ago when the sandbag fell?

Donald Tompkins shrank back. His lower lip trembled. Nancy leaned forward to hear how he would defend himself against Nora's accusation.

Abruptly the whiny young man whirled around and scooted away. He sprang off the curb, jaywalking across the busy street.

Poised to chase the man, Nancy asked Nora, "Is he really a stalker?"

"Virtually," the composer replied with an airy wave of her hand.

Nancy relaxed and let Donald duck around the corner out of sight. Her blue eyes darkening, she asked, "What do you mean, 'virtually'?"

"For the past three years he has attached himself like a leech to Marta Willentz," Nora said. "He's in the audience during every performance; he haunts the stage door during every intermission. I'm told he writes her a fan letter every single day."

"Has she notified the police?" Nancy asked.

Nora looked surprised. "No. After all, he's her biggest fan."

"Surely this is more than being a fan," Nancy said. She traded concerned looks with Bess, who was propping the stage door open with her foot. "Stalkers can be dangerous."

Nora chuckled. "This is the opera world, my dear. Every important singer has devoted fans like that. Big stars like Marta may have several."

Bess shivered. "Sounds creepy to me."

Nora shrugged. "Depends on your point of view. Opera stars need their fans as much as the fans need them. Singers work and sacrifice for years to succeed in this very specialized business. They deserve someone to adore them, to toss them bouquets onstage, to mob them at the stage door—to be their groupies, if you will. The fans perform that function. In return, fans earn a place in the opera community they love, even if they haven't a shred of musical talent."

Nora saw a taxicab approaching and raised a hand to hail it. "Marta would be devastated if Donald stopped following her," she said. "It would convince her that she was washed up. May he always be around!" And with that, Nora hopped into the cab.

Nancy and Bess went back inside, mulling over what Nora had told them. "One thing Lauren Sweet said is definitely right," Nancy muttered to her friend. "This place *is* full of wackos."

As they returned to the costume area, another woman stood chatting with Lauren. She was a matronly type of woman with drab brown hair, and she was wearing a plain white blouse and slacks. "There you are, girls," Lauren greeted them. "Meet Greta Lindbaum, Marta Willentz's dresser."

"Dresser?" Bess asked.

"Principal singers have their own people to help them with costumes, wigs, and makeup," Greta explained in a quiet, soothing voice. "I have been exclusively with Marta for eight years now."

"Oh, then you must know this Donald Thompson guy," Bess said.

"Donald Tompkins," Greta said. "Dear Donald. So loyal to Marta. She has several devoted followers, of course, but Donald is special. After every performance, he sends a present to Marta's dressing room." A smile flickered across her face at the thought. "It's always some kind of butterfly."

"She likes butterflies?" Nancy guessed.

"Not particularly," Greta said. "But it refers to her

trademark role." Noting the blank look on Nancy's face, she added, "*Madame Butterfly*, the Puccini opera."

"Oh, right!" Nancy made the connection.

"I know it's silly, but over the years Marta has come to expect her butterfly gifts," Greta went on. "She was quite upset when some of them disappeared from her dressing room two weeks ago."

Nancy recalled Mr. Reynolds mentioning such a theft. "Stolen?"

Greta nodded. "So it seems. It's mystifying. Those butterflies were mere trifles. They had sentimental value only to Marta. The same with the jewelry that disappeared from her case; the thief passed over the expensive stuff to take an enamel brooch and garnet necklace that Marta especially loved. They were gifts from her former husband."

Nancy was about to pry further into Marta's past when the stage manager's voice came booming down the hall. "All chorus members, onstage immediately! We're ready for the wedding scene."

"Ooh, that's us," Bess said, grabbing Nancy's arm. "We'll get the other costumes at our next break. Okay, Lauren?"

"Yeah, you'd better hurry," Lauren said, nudging Nancy from the other side. "Doug will bite your head off if you're late!"

Considering that her chorus role was her cover,

Nancy had no choice. "See you later," she called to Greta Lindbaum as Bess herded her away.

Over the next three hours, Nancy quickly came to appreciate what a big undertaking an opera production could be. There were four different groups of people milling about onstage: the stars, the small corps of ballerinas, the chorus, and the extras. And each group had a different agenda.

Since the extras weren't familiar with the opera production, they took up a large part of Steven Reynolds's attention. "No, downstage—*downstage!*" he scolded one clumsy young man carrying a rake. "Haven't you ever been onstage before? You hold it in the other hand, the one closest to the audience."

The young man blushed and shifted the rake to his other hand. "Sorry, Mr. Reynolds," he mumbled.

"Bess, isn't that Mark Stephens?" Nancy whispered. "You know, from our class in high school?"

"You're right, it is!" Bess exclaimed. "I heard he was taking a year off before college—something about becoming eligible for football. It's funny to see him here. I never knew he was interested in opera."

Nancy grinned. "When he sees us, he'll be plenty surprised. He never knew we were interested in opera either!"

For an hour or so, the scene seemed incredibly chaotic to Nancy. Along with the singers, dancers, chorus, and extras, there was a handful of musicians in the orchestra pit. It was half of the usual orchestra, just enough to play cues for the singers.

Suddenly the flow of people onstage began to make sense. Even though they were dressed in everyday modern clothes, they somehow began to move and act like a crowd of eighteenth-century country peasants.

Nancy looked up from the sheaf of music someone had thrust into her hands. She spotted a satisfied look on Reynolds's face. "Now you're getting it, people," he called out over the singing. "Rosa, are you ready?"

"Si, signore." Nancy heard the soprano call out in Italian from the wings.

As the music swelled, Rosacrucia Alba promenaded onstage. She was in full costume. Nancy detected a ripple of surprise in the voices around her. Nobody else was in costume. *What is Rosa up to?* she wondered. Was she that intent on showing off her tiny waist?

Nancy looked over at Marta, who was seated as the countess beside Sean Torrance, the count. She squared her shoulders, looking confident but offended. She was clearly angry about the way her costar was showing off.

Rosa spun around with an extra swish of her cream-colored chiffon skirt. She swished her hips directly at Sean Torrance. The astounded baritone gaped at her.

Rosa tossed her mane of black hair, clasped her hands in front of her waist, and began to execute a series of trills. Her full red lips moved open and closed as she guided her bell-like voice higher and higher. The chorus fell silent and parted to give Rosa full command of the stage.

Though Nancy didn't know the music, she could tell when the aria was approaching its final crescendo. All eyes were upon Rosa. With a glint in her dark eyes, she drew one more huge breath.

Just then everybody heard the loud *pop!* The crisscrossed golden laces of Rosa's bodice went springing every which way. The seams of her chiffon dress burst open, revealing creamy white skin beneath.

And as Rosa hit her high note her beautiful wedding gown slid down to the stage floor.

5

She Who Laughs Last

Nancy would never forget the look of shock and shame on Rosacrucia Alba's face. With a mortified scream, she reached down to snatch up her dress.

It was too late, of course. Everybody had already seen her in her petticoat. The once-hushed chorus tried to contain giggles.

Rosa clutched her ruined dress around her and rushed off stage. Steven Reynolds threw down his baton and followed her. The chorus members couldn't contain themselves anymore. Laughter filled the room.

Nancy looked across stage at Marta Willentz. The soprano's face shone with a look of triumph. Nancy felt uneasy. *I guess you can't blame her for enjoying*

Rosa's humiliation, she thought. *But she looks almost smug about it.*

Nancy began to head offstage, but Bess caught up with her. "Where are you going? We haven't finished the scene. When Mr. Reynolds comes back—"

"He'll understand why I left," Nancy assured her friend. She slipped into the wings and through the stage doorway, into the brick hallway. She wasn't surprised to see George pop out from the door that led to the auditorium. She knew her friend had witnessed the entire incident from her seat in the mezzanine.

George gestured toward a succession of dark-green dressing-room doors lining the corridor. "Which one is Rosa's dressing room?" she asked.

"I know a good way to find out," Nancy said. Leaning close to each door to listen, she worked her way down the right side of the hall, while George took the left. Behind the fourth door, Nancy heard agitated voices. She waved George over.

Behind the door, the girls heard Rosa Alba's voice, its musical sweetness turned to a vicious snarl. "If you had been here to inspect the dress, this would never have happened."

"But Rosacrucia!" A female voice was protesting.

"Wait, wait," Reynolds broke in. "You weren't even here, Paula? Where were you?"

"I didn't mean to be late," the other woman declared. Her voice quivered, as though she were close to tears. "I couldn't help it. My rental car had a flat tire. I couldn't get here from the hotel until the road service came to fix it."

Nancy looked at George. "Can you check that out?" she whispered. George nodded and jogged off.

Nancy kept her ear to the door. "What sort of an excuse is that?" Rosa hissed. "If your tire is flat, then you leave the car, take a taxi, and get here. Somehow. I needed you!"

"It wasn't a dress rehearsal," Paula said.

"I don't care. You are Paula Konstance, the dresser of Rosacrucia Alba. You should always be here." Rosa was furious.

"Rosa, darling, give her a break," Steven coaxed her. "Paula's been with you for several years now. Her devotion has never been a question."

Nancy, hearing footsteps behind her, swiftly moved away from the door. She turned to see Lauren Sweet running up the hall. "I just heard what happened," she said to Nancy. "Is Rosa upset?"

"That would be an understatement," Nancy said. "She's practically hysterical."

"Poor woman," Lauren said, turning the doorknob. She cracked open the door and stuck her head in. "Can I help?"

"Oh, Lauren, thank goodness you're here," Steven said. "Something went wrong with Rosa's third act costume for *Figaro*."

As Lauren stepped inside the dressing room Nancy boldly slipped in behind her. Lauren took the costume in both hands, shook aside the flounces of chiffon and satin, and bent over the torn bodice. "Did you have on that bone corset I gave you?" she asked Rosa.

Rosa shook her head defiantly. "That bulky thing made me look fatter, not thinner."

Lauren frowned. "The strings on this bodice were pulled so tight, your ribcage was straining against it. When they popped, your ribcage expanded. That's what burst the dress seams." She bit her lip. Nancy guessed she'd decided not to remind Rosa that she'd warned her not to tie the bodice so tight.

Nancy sidled quietly over to the costumer. Lauren handed her Rosa's dress, pointing to the frayed fabric around the seams. Then she held up the velvet bodice with its dangling gold laces. Nancy inspected the bodice laces. They had broken at the back, inside the bodice, not in front where they crisscrossed.

She studied the broken ends. All of them were cleanly severed, angling down to a few ripped threads at the edge. From the looks of it, someone had sliced the laces almost to the edge, then left them—knowing that they would eventually break under the strain onstage.

Nancy looked up, forgetting to be subtle. "Who handled this costume today?" she asked.

Rosa looked at her vaguely, as if trying to figure out who she was. "I was wearing it earlier—I took it off to have a shower . . ." Her eyes narrowed. "I left the costume lying all alone, because my *dresser* couldn't bother to be here."

Paula Konstance burst into tears. Rosa crossed her arms and turned her back on her devoted assistant.

Steven put his arm around the soprano. "Rosa, darling, why don't you go back to your hotel and rest? This has been very upsetting for you, I know. You can skip the rest of rehearsal today."

Rosa flashed him an angry glance. "What? And leave Marta and Sean and the others to gloat over my shame?"

Steven suppressed a sigh. "They'll be sent home too. We'll just make it a technical run-through with the stage crew, chorus, and extras."

Rosa plopped down at her dressing table and began to brush her dark hair with angry strokes. "I suppose so," she said huffily. "Paula, drive me to the hotel. That is, if your car is finally working now."

Steven seized the moment to leave the dressing room. Lauren and Nancy slipped out behind him. "Paula will get her calmed down now," Steven said once they were safely in the hall with the door closed. "She's very good at that."

"She's had enough practice," Lauren said with a

wry smile. "But seriously, Steven, I don't know what happened. That bodice was okay this morning."

"The laces had been cut," Nancy announced. "Someone tampered with it."

Steven looked stricken. "Another sabotage?"

Nancy nodded. "We have to find out who had access to the costume this afternoon. The question is, who would want to do it? And why?"

"To humiliate Rosa?" Lauren suggested.

"Most of the company has a motive to do that," Steven admitted. "Well, at least no one was really hurt. And it was only a rehearsal—I can't imagine how awful it would have been for Rosa if that had happened in a real performance." He gave Nancy an uneasy look.

"I'd better go get things back on track," Steven added in a distracted mutter. He strode off, calling out, "Doug? Strike the *Figaro* set and bring on the *Aida* scenery!"

"Come on, Nancy, let me give you your *Aida* costume," Lauren said.

Nancy followed her to the wardrobe area, where she tried on the white linen sheath of an Egyptian townsperson. Lauren showed her how to tuck the folds of the sheath into a gold vinyl belt, then top it off with a neckplate encrusted with fake jewels. "Nobody in ancient Egypt had your color of hair," Lauren said, "but instead of a black wig, cover it up with this." She set a clinging gold headdress on Nancy's red-blond hair.

Nancy smiled, fingering the small golden serpent coiled over her forehead. "This is fun."

"It looks great," Lauren said. "Now go hang it in your numbered space on the racks, next to your *Figaro* costume, so you can find it tomorrow."

"We chorus extras don't have our own dressers," Nancy joked. "By the way, Lauren . . . do you think Paula Konstance might have cut Rosa's bodice?"

Lauren shook her head firmly. "No way. Paula's very dedicated, very professional. And she adores Rosa. Usually Rosa's kind to Paula—stars need the loyalty of their dressers, you see, and Rosa does know how loyal Paula is. She was only rude today because she was upset."

When Nancy returned to the stage, it was buzzing with activity. Stagehands swarmed over the catwalk and the wings, practicing set changes. Nancy stepped aside just in time to avoid being hit by a painted palm tree being lowered into place on the left side of the stage.

Just then she heard a stagehand she'd met earlier, Mike Cordasco, growling as he shoved a plaster statue into place. "This is the second time you got it wrong, Jackie," he was scolding the young female stagehand. "You weren't in place at the top of the second act of *Figaro*, either."

Nancy looked around the edge of the palm tree to see Jackie Ahern cringing beside the statue. "I told you, I was in the set shop repairing a garland of fake flowers."

"That's not good enough," Mike said, shaking his head. "Look, I'm trying to protect you from Doug noticing your mistakes, but there's only so much I can do. One more strike and you're surely going to be out."

As Mike stomped away Nancy saw Jackie drop her head and take a miserable punch at the statue. Nancy felt sorry for her.

"*Aida* extras, center stage!" Steven Reynolds called out. Nancy hurried to join the straggling clump of temporary cast members. "Now, here's the setup," Steven told them. "You women are part of a typical street crowd, cheering the victorious Egyptian army as they return to Memphis from defeating the Ethiopians. You're singing a hymn to the goddess Isis. Men, you fill in the ranks of the soldiers."

Bess nudged Nancy and pointed to their old classmate, Mark Stephens, practicing marching. Nancy had to admit, he was doing it with gusto. The trouble was, his lumbering walk looked more like the football player he was than the disciplined Egyptian soldier he was playing.

"That's great, soldiers," Reynolds said. "Remember, you've just won a big battle. Strut and look superior." As Reynolds turned away, Nancy saw Mark Stephens grin and add a goofy little end-zone dance on the fake parapets at the edge of the stage.

Mark's antics were still on Nancy's mind an hour later, during a break, when Steven Reynolds finally had time to talk to her. Just as she opened her mouth to tell Reynolds about Mark's strange goofing off, Nancy noticed something else unusual.

A woman in a chic gray suit was approaching Nancy and Steven, followed by a gaggle of visitors with cameras and notepads. Nancy guessed they were reporters from local papers. "Marta Willentz and Rosa Alba will sing in two operas each," the woman was explaining. "And they're such fierce rivals, they're determined to outshine each other."

Nancy saw Steven Reynold's jaw tighten. "Oh, no. If all this backstage drama gets into the papers, the board of directors will find out, and they'll have my head on a platter!" he groaned.

He thrust Nancy aside and hurried over to the press tour. "Sara, what kind of public relations is this?" he said.

"Oh, Steven, I was just telling the members of the press about the tension between our two sopranos," the woman said brightly. "Their River Heights performances will surely be really intense."

The reporters eagerly jotted down the gossip item the publicist had given them. Nancy saw Steven Reynolds sink his head into his hands.

6

A Cast of Suspects

The publicist turned to look at Steven. "What's wrong?" she asked innocently.

But the damage had already been done. Steven smiled weakly at the reporters. "Miss Tucci exaggerates," he said. "Of course Marta Willentz and Rosa Alba want to give great performances—they always do. And they have a cordial professional relationship. Now please take a seat and watch us rehearse the death scene from *Aida*."

"With Miss Alba? She's playing Aida, isn't she?" a reporter asked.

Steven pushed his glasses back up his nose. "I'm afraid she is at her hotel resting her voice. This is just a technical run-through. Now please, find a seat and get comfortable."

He caught Sara Tucci's arm as the reporters headed for the auditorium. "What were you thinking?" he hissed angrily. "With all the trouble around here lately, why make our lives more difficult by drawing attention to the competition between those two singers?"

Sara looked confused. "A human interest angle always brings in the crowds. That's what I'm hired to do—bring in the crowds."

"Did you stop to think how Rosa or Marta would feel, reading that rumor in the papers?"

Sara winced. "I guess not. But Nora Stubbs suggested it. She said the story would generate publicity."

"Nora Stubbs—that pest!" Steven roared. Without another word, he stormed off.

Early the next morning, over coffee at a cute little café near the theater, Nancy told George and Bess about Steven's flare-up in front of the press. "I must say, I thought he overreacted," she said.

"He has to be sensitive to publicity," Bess reasoned. "It's a big responsibility to run a road tour for the country's top opera company."

"Also, bad press could make Marta and Rosa go nuts," George added. "They're his headliners; without them, he has no show."

Nancy wasn't convinced. "I talked this over with my dad this morning," she said. "He pointed out that the American Grand Opera has such a huge reputation, people would come no matter who was singing. I have to wonder if Steven has another motive for shushing this up."

Bess leaned forward. "You suspect Steven Reynolds, Nan?"

Nancy shrugged. "I'm not saying he caused any of these accidents, but he may know more than he lets on. Still, it's just a hunch. Let's try to line up some hard facts. George, what did you get on Paula Konstance yesterday?"

"She was telling the truth. She did have a flat tire, and she waited for the road service to fix it," George reported. "The desk clerk at the River Heights Inn verified that. But when I finally tracked down the mechanic this morning, guess what? He says her tire had been slashed."

Nancy sat up. "So someone gave her that flat tire on purpose. I wonder who—and why?"

"The mechanic says usually kids do that," George said. "But the parking lot at that inn is too well guarded for casual pranksters to get in."

Nancy was jotting notes on a small pocket notepad. "Anybody from the company could have been in the parking lot," she said.

"The River Heights Inn?" Bess repeated. "But most everyone is staying at the Regent Hotel, just across the street from the theater."

"How do you know that?" George asked.

Bess blushed. "Well, this cute tenor in the chorus asked me to a party there last night. I didn't go, but I remembered which hotel."

Nancy tapped her cheek with her pen. "Why is Paula staying at the River Heights Inn instead?"

"Seems obvious to me," George said. "Paula stays wherever Rosa stays, right? And you can bet Rosa won't stay in the same hotel as Marta."

"Good deduction," Nancy said. "But Bess, ask around today and find out for sure." She scanned her notepad. "Whoever prevented Paula from getting to the rehearsal . . ."

"I bet it was the same person who cut Rosa's corset strings," Bess said.

"Possibly," Nancy said. "What time did the desk clerk say Paula discovered her flat tire?"

"One o'clock," George said. "The mechanic arrived at two, and once it was fixed, she had a twenty-minute drive to the theater."

"And when did we see Rosa in the wardrobe area?" Nancy asked Bess.

"About twelve thirty," Bess recalled.

Nancy did some quick math in her head. "Then her bodice had to be cut between twelve thirty and two, when Rosa went onstage to rehearse. He or she could have cut the laces at twelve thirty, driven twenty minutes to the inn, and slashed the tire just before Paula saw her car."

"But only if Rosa took off her costume right after we saw her," Bess said.

"It's more likely that the culprit slashed the tires first, well before one o'clock," George said. "He or she could be back at the theater by one thirty and have time to cut the laces before Rosa dressed for rehearsal."

"It would still be close," Nancy said. "I'm beginning to think we're looking at a two-person crime. And that opens the door to a lot more suspects."

"Like who?" Bess asked.

Nancy sighed. "Like Marta Willentz, for one. It's true that she couldn't have dropped the sandbag from the catwalk yesterday; she was standing in plain sight on center stage when it fell. But if she was working with an accomplice . . ."

"But why would Marta steal things from her own dressing room?" George asked. "And didn't you say Marta was being stalked?"

Nancy pushed her empty coffee cup away. "What if these incidents weren't all done by the same person? For all we know, both Rosa and Marta are playing ugly pranks on each other. Or it could be someone with a grudge against the American Grand Opera itself. Sabotaging the stars is just one way to hurt the company."

"How will we keep investigating? We'll be stuck onstage all day. We're rehearsing this morning, and have a matinee this afternoon," Bess grumbled as she got up.

"Onstage is where the action seems to be," Nancy declared. "Although if you can spend the day doing some research, George—"

"Consider it done," George said as they left the café. "Who should I check up on?"

"Everybody," Nancy said. "Marta and Rosa, of course; I'd go online and get some background information about them. They're big stars, so there should be plenty of material. Sean Torrance, too; I'm eager to know the history of his association with Marta. And then there's Nora Stubbs. She might very well have reason for revenge on the opera company, or on one singer. Don't forget to get Reynolds's history too."

"He would *never* sabotage his own opera company," Bess protested. "He has a lot to lose if this tour tanks."

"I hope George's research will prove that," Nancy said. "And George, try running a few other names on an Internet search. Paula Konstance, for one." Her steps slowed as they neared the stage door. "And Donald Tompkins."

George looked baffled. "Who?"

Nancy glanced around the stage door area before she replied, "Marta's number one fan. If there's anything suspicious in his past . . ."

She didn't need to finish the thought. Bess and George had worked with her on enough cases before. They knew what dangers she foresaw.

Even Nancy began to feel the pump of adrenaline as the extras gathered in the wings that afternoon, before Act Two, scene two, of Giuseppe Verdi's great opera *Aida*. Even watching the first act on the grainy closed-circuit TV in the green room—the cast's waiting lounge—had been thrilling. The idea that she was actually going to be onstage in an opera was finally hitting Nancy.

"Is my headdress on straight, Bess?" she asked her friend.

"Yep, the serpent's right in place," Bess said. The headdress she wore over her blond curls was equally beautiful, with a glittering sun motif.

A few yards away, Nancy saw Steven Reynolds pull Mark Stephens aside. *Good,* Nancy thought.

Just then Rosa Alba materialized from the wings. In her clinging *Aida* costume, she looked slinky and provocative. Rosa strolled over to Mark, twined her hands around his muscular football-player arms, and gazed up at him flirtatiously.

Nancy pushed through the crowd toward the pair, but by the time she reached Mark, Rosa had vanished. "Wow, Mark, the star of the show talked to you," Nancy said, trying to keep her tone light. "What did she say?"

"Oh, that?" Mark said with a conceited jut of his jaw. "No big deal. She said I was the only guy here who really looks like a fighting man."

And you bought it, Nancy thought.

The first bars of the scene's music rang out. Nancy leaped into place and paraded onstage with the others, but she had a queasy feeling. She could tell that Rosa's attention had gone to Mark's head. There was no telling what he would do now, with that new confidence.

As the curtain rose Nancy gazed out at the audience, transfixed. She'd been onstage before, but never in a performance this grand. The gorgeous music seemed to transform everything; the cutout palm trees and the fake jeweled headdresses melted into a shimmering vision of ancient Egypt. Nancy mouthed the words to the music and gestured broadly, caught up in the power of the scene.

Soon the soldiers marched in, their sandaled feet perfectly in step. On cue, Nancy bowed down to honor the troops, touching her forehead to the stage floor.

As she rose she caught sight of Mark. He was still overacting, despite Steven's warning. Pumping his spear into the air, he starting dancing backward, cocking his shoulders from side to side. Nancy froze, helpless, as Mark edged closer and closer to the end of the papier-mâché parapet.

As though in slow motion, she saw his foot slide off the crumbling rim of fake stonework. He lurched, trying to catch himself—but his momentum was too great.

Nancy lunged forward, but she was too late: Mark had already tipped over the edge of the stage.

7

Sabotage!

It was a long way down to the floor of the orchestra pit. Nancy knew Mark was falling right into the cello section. She couldn't see what happened, but she heard a woman cry out in pain, and the sound of wood snapping. *Was that a cello?* Nancy thought.

A gasp of horror rose from the audience. The orchestra made a few last dissonant squeaks before stopping altogether. In the wings, Nancy saw Doug, the stage manager, frantically gesture across his throat with his forefinger—the universal sign for *cut!* A stagehand leaped to the curtain pulleys. The main curtain came hurtling down.

Nancy, already close to the front edge of the stage, spread out her arms to pin back as much as she could of the curious chorus. Mike Cordasco, wearing black clothes to minimize the chances of him being seen during scene changes, knelt beside the parapet. Mark's fall had severely damaged the fake stonework.

Nancy saw Mike scratch his head. "How'd it break?" she asked in a low tone.

"Darnedest thing," Mike murmured. "I rebuilt this set myself yesterday; modified it to go over the raised lip on this stage. I put on a heavy steel hinge so we could hook it over the edge of the pit. And now the hinge is missing. The screw holes aren't torn, like they would be if it'd been pulled out. The hinge was unscrewed and removed."

Nancy searched his face. She saw the pride of a good craftsman and guessed he was already redesigning it in his mind, step by step.

Steven pushed through the crowd. "How did this happen?" he demanded.

Mike stood up. "Faulty carpentry, I guess," he said stolidly. "A hinge gave out."

"Jackie was up here fiddling with the set right before the curtain," said another stagehand beside Mike.

Steven looked concerned. "The new stagehand? Where is she?"

"Here," piped up Jackie's quiet voice. The curious chorus members, drinking in the drama, made room for Jackie to join Steven.

"Were you tampering with the set?" Steven demanded.

Jackie looked like a frightened deer. "Not *tampering.* I was adjusting it. Mr. Torrance told me it looked loose, so I came out to check. I knew Mike would be upset if it broke."

Mike threw his hands up into the air. "Singers!" he exclaimed. "Do we question how they sing? Never. But when they pick on our work—"

Steven held up a hand to silence him. "I'll speak to Sean," he said.

"No way was that set loose," Doug broke in. "It was that crazy kid hopping around on it. We didn't build this thing to support human weight, especially not a big guy like him."

Steven took off his glasses and rubbed his forehead. "He refused to follow the scene blocking. I spoke to him about it twice. But some things are beyond my control, apparently." He slid his glasses back on, stepped to the part in the curtain, and peered out at the auditorium. "Good, the ambulance crew has come for that extra and the cellist. The show must go on. I'll go speak to the audience and then raise the curtain. We'll take it from Carol's stanza."

Nodding and murmuring, the chorus members moved back into their places.

Nancy, however, had no intention of joining them.

She followed Mike Cordasco offstage into the wings. "Mister Cordasco? Could I speak to you for a minute?"

The stagehand turned, giving her white sheath and headdress a curious look. "Aren't you supposed to be onstage?"

She made an impatient gesture. "The guy who got hurt is a friend of mine. I want to explain to him how this happened."

Mike curled his lip into a cynical smile. "It happened because he ignored the director's blocking. Tell him that."

Nancy held her ground. "But someone told me there was another scenery collapse recently. Isn't that an odd coincidence?"

Mike's jaw tightened. "It sure is. Believe me, our set crew has a super-clean safety record. Not once in our time together have we seen two accidents in a week."

Nancy sensed she had rattled his pride as well as his anger. She judged she could push it only a tiny bit further. "Tell me about the other accident. Was that a set you built too?"

Mike sighed. "I do structural stuff, tricky pieces that need real engineering. The other piece was a simple backdrop. It fell over, that's all."

Nancy was skeptical. "Backdrops don't just fall over," she said.

Mike's eyes glinted in the dim light. "You're right. Here, let me show you."

He led Nancy deeper backstage, where huge painted flats were stacked eight or ten deep against the high walls. "Each one has these wooden struts on the back," he demonstrated to her. "This is the piece that fell. It's the cathedral background for *Tosca,* in Act One. Look here."

He whipped out a small flashlight and pointed its beam at a series of simple plywood triangles, which were nailed to the back of a huge square frame that had a sheet of painted canvas stretched over it. Nancy was amazed that such a simple piece of scenery could create the sort of dazzling illusion she'd seen tonight.

"That's where it broke," Mike continued, indicating a thin line that bisected the wooden support. "We glued it back together."

Nancy squatted down and squinted at the plywood strut. "It's a clean break, not a jagged tear. It looks like somebody sawed that support in half." Something about the cut bothered her, but she couldn't place what it was.

Mike snapped off the flashlight. "Same thing I saw. I told Doug, and I guess he told Reynolds. But did they do anything about it? Nope."

"Well, one thing we know," Nancy said, sitting back on her heels. "Jackie Ahern couldn't have done this. She wasn't even on the crew until a couple days ago, right?"

A smile broke onto Mike's face. "That's true. I'm glad you pointed that out. I hate to see the kid get in trouble. First the fallen sandbag, now this—and she's trying so hard to learn the ropes."

Nancy thanked the stagehand for his information and left him there amid his beloved sets. But as she returned to the main stage area, her face darkened with concern.

This afternoon's incident proved to her that, without a doubt, there was sabotage afoot. Granted, Mark shouldn't have gone onto the set. But someone had made sure that that parapet wouldn't hold up.

Then Nancy thought of Rosa's corset strings, which had been nearly completely cut—the same way that the support had been sawed. *Perhaps that same person planned for Rosa's bodice to burst open in* Figaro *tonight,* she mused. No one had expected Rosa to wear the costume in rehearsal yesterday.

Finding herself in the brick hallway, Nancy turned toward the line of dressing rooms on one side. She wanted to hear what Sean Torrance had to say about the broken set. Act Two was almost over; he should be returning to his dressing room soon.

Outside the door, she was startled to see Nora Stubbs. "What are you doing here?" Nancy asked.

Nora smiled wryly. "You mean because Steven

was mad at me yesterday about Sara's publicity angle? I'm not worried. I knew he'd be mad at someone else by now. I hear Sean's the culprit of the moment, for telling that stagehand to meddle with the set."

Nancy was impressed by Nora's ability to pick up information. *Maybe I can use her on this case,* she thought. "I guess the stagehands were mad at him for meddling," she said.

"Sean makes enemies on the crew," Nora scoffed. "He complains so often that he's a joke. Even if he said nothing, they'd blame it on him."

"And you believe that girl instead of me?" Nancy heard Sean's baritone voice boom nearby.

Sean came striding down the hallway, Steven Reynolds tagging along at his side. Tall, handsome Sean cut a striking figure, dressed in the torn robes of the captured Ethiopian king Amonasro.

"I'm not blaming you," Steven said. "But there was an accident, and I have to get to the bottom of it. Did you speak to Jackie about the set?"

"The set was stupidly designed, Steven," Sean replied. "Why make it stick out so far? And your stage blocking was confusing. Yes, I did say something to that stagehand." He reached out for the water bottle an assistant was handing him and took a long swig.

"I wouldn't complain on my own account," Sean

added. "I wasn't due to walk onto the parapet. But Rosa was. A few minutes later, and it could have been her in that orchestra pit. How would you have liked that?"

Nancy pressed herself against the wall as Sean and Steven brushed past her. Her mind jumped to an image of Rosa, encouraging Mark's ridiculous moves. Had she used him to take the fall for her? Had she known about the parapet?

Nancy slipped into Steven's office to wait for him. Possibilities swirled in her mind. How had Sean learned the set was loose? Why had that other stagehand ratted on Jackie for adjusting the parapet? And why was Nora Stubbs hanging around?

Sitting at Steven's desk, Nancy glanced at the files piled on a corner. One of them was labeled PERSONNEL. Nancy idly picked it up. Maybe she could supplement George's research with information from these files. She felt sure Steven wouldn't mind her reading them; after all, he *had* asked her to snoop around.

The top paper inside the file was a job application: Jackie Ahern's. *That's natural,* Nancy thought, *since Jackie is the company's most recent hire.* Nancy skimmed the sheet of paper.

Jackie had a River Heights address and phone number, and under the SCHOOLING heading she had written that she'd graduated from River Heights

High, in the class six years before Nancy's. *Funny I never heard of her,* Nancy thought.

All the previous jobs Jackie listed were at small theaters around San Francisco. *Why has Jackie come back to River Heights?* Nancy thought. There weren't exactly loads of theater jobs in town.

Nancy found a sheet of paper and copied the names of Jackie's references from the application. It wouldn't hurt to have George check them out.

From the subsiding bustle in the hallway, Nancy guessed that the intermission was almost over. Steven must be too busy to stop by his office. *Never mind,* Nancy thought. While the singers were onstage, the set crew would be hanging around—and that gave her an idea. She picked up the phone on Steven's desk and dialed a number she knew by heart: Rocco's Pizzeria.

Half an hour later, Nancy had changed back into jeans and a sweater and met the delivery guy from Rocco's at the stage door. Carrying the pizza carton, Nancy wandered into the scenery storeroom.

As she'd hoped, Nancy spotted Jackie Ahern sitting alone on a stack of wooden pallets. She was reading. "Hi, Jackie," Nancy said. "Remember me—Nancy? We met yesterday. I'm one of the extras."

Jackie looked up from her book, frowning. "Nancy? Hmm, I don't remember . . ."

Nancy didn't give Jackie time to finish. "I'm not in

this act, so I ordered dinner. This is too much pizza for me. Want some?"

"I guess," Jackie said warily.

Nancy set the box on the pallets and opened it. "Too bad about that guy playing the soldier, Mark Stephens. He was in my class at school. Did you go to River Heights High?"

"Yes," Jackie said. "But a while ago."

"What were you doing before this?" Nancy asked, handing Jackie a slice.

"A little here, a little there," Jackie said. She blew on the slice to cool it. "Not many stage jobs in town. I'm lucky this one came along, even if it's only temporary." She bit into the pizza. "This is good."

"It's from Rocco's," Nancy said. "You know Rocco's? Over on, uh, Marvin Street?"

"Sure," Jackie said. "I always go there."

Nancy took a bite, but her stomach churned. If Jackie were from River Heights, she'd have known that Rocco's was on Main Street. There wasn't any Marvin Street in River Heights.

Why was she lying?

8

A Chilling Silence

I can't let Jackie see that I know she's lying, Nancy thought. She'd learned that suspects were more likely to betray themselves if they had no idea they were suspects.

"How'd you hear about this job?" Nancy asked, leaning against the wooden pallets.

"Well, I read in the paper that the opera was coming to town," Jackie said.

"In the *River Heights Clarion?*" Nancy asked.

Jackie nodded. *Another strike against you,* Nancy thought. Anyone from town knew that the local paper was the *River Heights Gazette.*

"I love opera," Jackie went on. "When I came to buy my tickets, I saw a sign saying 'Stagehand Needed,' so I applied."

"Wasn't that lucky?" Nancy said. "You were here just when they needed someone. But why did they need a new stagehand this late in the tour?"

"Someone had an accident," Jackie said. "It happened in the town before this one on the tour: Preston City."

Nancy tossed her pizza crust back into the box. "And when the guy gets better?"

Jackie shrugged. "They'll give him his job back and I'll be out. Mr. Reynolds made that clear when he hired me." She then added with a rueful smile, "I haven't exactly scored points with the stage crew. No one's nice to me, except Mike. They aren't used to working with women, I guess."

"So I noticed," Nancy said sympathetically. "Want another piece of pizza?"

"No thanks, I'm full." Jackie stood up and stretched her thin, boyish body. "But I appreciate it. I've been kinda lonely here." Her pale gray eyes focused on Nancy. "What's your name again? I'm terrible with names."

"Nancy."

"Well, see you around then, Nancy." Jackie wandered back into the scenery shop.

Nancy glanced at the three-quarters of pizza left. Bess would help her finish it, she decided—and the pizza had been a good investment. If nothing else, her little chat with Jackie had convinced Nancy to add the stagehand to her suspect list.

Bess and Nancy tried to look casual by eating pizza in the green room while they eavesdropped on the talk swirling around. Chorus members had taken off their Egyptian costumes and were lounging around in shorts and T-shirts, enjoying a break before suiting up for that night's performance of *Tosca.* Nancy kept watching the door for Steven to enter, but he must have been busy elsewhere.

He did, however, send Sara Tucci with news from the hospital: neither Mark Stephens nor the cellist, Yvonne Hicks, had been badly hurt by the fall earlier. Nancy sensed a general sigh of relief, as if everyone in the company had been more shaken by the accident than they had let on. But Sara looked very stressed. Nancy guessed she was already busy struggling to put a positive public spin on the incident.

Soon the pre-performance bustle began for the evening show. Act One of *Tosca* was set in a cathedral, when the artist Cavaradossi is painting a fresco. Nancy and Bess, dressed as nuns in long black habits and white wimples, were assigned to walk across stage halfway through the act. They reappeared later, as part of a religious celebration.

When the time arrived for them to walk onstage, Nancy stole a nervous glance at the painted cathedral backdrop. *Let's hope Mike's repairs will keep it steady tonight,* she thought.

The cast had rehearsed *Tosca* yesterday after the principal singers left, so Nancy had not yet heard Marta Willentz—playing Cavaradossi's love, the spirited singer Floria Tosca—in her first-act aria "Non la sospiri." Nancy stood transfixed while Marta sang. David Landers, the tenor who sang Cavaradossi, had two gorgeous arias as well. "Puccini was an amazing composer," Nancy whispered to Bess as they moved offstage.

"He's my favorite," Bess agreed.

"That's what you said about Verdi this afternoon—and about Mozart yesterday," Nancy said, gently punching her friend in the arm.

Bess smiled. "I can't help it. All of these operas have so much beautiful music in them."

Nancy pushed up the long black sleeve of her nun costume to check her watch. In twenty minutes they were due back onstage. "Let's go to the green room," she suggested to Bess. "My throat's parched." But the look she threw Bess signaled that it was really information she was after—not water.

Once they entered the green room, Nancy halted. Rosa was perched on a long sofa with Sara Tucci and a dark-haired woman. Nancy knew Rosa didn't appear in tonight's opera. Shouldn't she be at her hotel, though, resting her voice?

Rosa, dressed in a dramatic dark green velvet caftan, waved a hand in the air. "Yes, *Aida* is a challenge to sing," she was saying. "But I feel a special empathy with Aida. She is far from her war-torn homeland of Ethiopia, as I am far from troubled Slovenia. And her love for the Egyptian captain, Radames, makes her a target for the jealousy of Princess Amneris."

The dark-haired woman raised her eyebrows. "And you, similarly, are in love with whom?"

Rosa's laugh was as musical as a silver bell. "I am not telling. Nor will I tell who is so jealous of me."

Sara Tucci laughed nervously as the woman scribbled on a notepad. "Margaret's from the *Chicago Sentinel,* Rosa. She's not really interested in personal anecdotes."

"Oh, yes, I am," the reporter declared. "These little tidbits will make Chicagoans want to buy tickets to the opera for next week."

Sara swallowed. Nancy, lingering at the water cooler, mused that Rosa obviously wasn't as opposed to gossipy publicity as Steven had assumed.

Rosa leaned back on the couch with an exaggerated look of innocence. "I am saying nothing, of course," she said. "It is such an honor for me just to appear onstage with an opera legend like Marta Willentz. Truly one of the great stars of the past."

Nancy and Bess exchanged glances. They both knew that Marta would hate to hear herself described like that.

"When she said she would sing the countess in *Figaro,*" Rosa continued, "I pleaded to sing Susanna's part beside her. How could I pass up that chance? It might be my last opportunity to perform with her. Who knows how much longer her voice will last?"

The reporter wrote down everything Rosa said, looking delighted to get such juicy quotes. Nancy murmured to Bess, "Steven said it was the other way around—that Rosa begged to sing Susanna first, then Marta fought her way in."

"Marta definitely won't be happy when this article hits the newsstands," Bess agreed.

Just then the stage manager stuck his head in the green room's doorway. "Extras, please get ready for the victory mass." Nancy wanted to eavesdrop on more of Rosa's interview, but Bess yanked on her arm to get her to return to the stage.

As Nancy and Bess filed onstage with a crowd of chorus members, Nancy mulled over Rosa's vicious games. *But that doesn't mean Marta's blameless,* Nancy warned herself, recalling the look of triumph on Marta's face when Rosa's dress burst open yesterday.

At that moment Tosca came back onstage. The

scheming villain, Scarpia, was showing her evidence that Cavaradossi was two-timing her. Nancy, kneeling in a fake pew nearby, glanced up and noticed the look of jealous fury possessing Marta's face.

Relax, Nancy, she's just acting, Nancy told herself. *Like Steven told you, Marta's a powerful actress as well as a singer.* But she still felt unnerved as Marta swept offstage, seemingly overcome by her passion.

As soon as the curtain fell, Nancy joined the scramble to empty the stage. Waves of applause rose as the principals took their bows, one at a time. Nancy paused near the stage to observe.

First, she saw Marta step through a part in the curtain. The audience went crazy. Amid frantic clapping came cries of "Brava! Brava! Bravissima!" Nancy loved the audience's exuberance.

Nancy saw Marta slip back behind the curtain, cradling bouquets of roses that had been tossed onstage for her. Her elegant face radiated joy. The jealous rage of a few moments ago *was* just an act, Nancy decided.

Gathering up the full skirt of her navy blue satin gown, Marta swept past Nancy and continued down the hall to her dressing room. Nancy followed.

Marta barely glanced at the chorus members and stage crew milling about. As she passed the doorway leading from backstage to the auditorium, a surging cluster of fans called out her name. She seemed oblivious, though. Nancy glimpsed Marta's obsessed fan Donald Tompkins, straining to get past the guard on duty.

Marta's dresser was waiting in the hall. She guided Marta into her dressing room and gave the door a resounding slam. The disappointed fans receded from the doorway.

Nancy turned to see Bess. "Come on, Nan, let's change out of these nun costumes," Bess said. "I was sweating buckets under those hot stage lights."

"Me too," Nancy admitted. "What I could use right now is a big, cold—"

Nancy was interrupted by a piercing scream of pain. It came from behind Marta Willentz's dressing room door!

9

The Show Must Go On

Nancy raced to Marta's door. Before she could get there, however, Steven popped out of another doorway. He flung open Marta's door. Nancy was right behind him.

Inside, she saw Marta Willentz huddled on a folding chair at her makeup mirror, gasping and crying with pain. Her motherly dresser, Greta Lindbaum, knelt beside her. "Her throat spray," Greta said, looking up at Steven. "Something strange must have been in it. It hurt her."

Over Marta's shoulder, Nancy saw a rubber squeeze bulb attached to the top of a small glass bottle of clear liquid. It was an old-fashioned atomizer.

Steven leaned solicitously over his star soprano. "Marta, dear," he said gently. "How do you feel?"

Marta twisted around with a look of total panic. She opened and closed her mouth, like a stranded fish on land. A few squeaks came from her throat.

Reynolds cringed, turning chalk-white. He gazed at her fiercely. "Can you . . . sing?"

Marta shook her head, her blue eyes brimming with fear.

Steven sank onto his knees, trembling. "How could this have happened? You were singing so beautifully. It was one of your finest performances ever!"

Tears trickled down Marta's cheeks, carving tracks in her heavy stage makeup. Her regal bearing was shattered. She clutched the director's arm, frantic with despair.

Steven looked bleakly at Nancy. The look in his eyes was clear. A few mishaps in rehearsals had been bad enough, but now a major star had been knocked out in the midst of a performance. There was no way to hide the company's troubles from the public—or from the board of directors. It was Steven Reynolds's worst nightmare.

Nancy could hear buzzing in the hallway beyond the half-open dressing room door. Already the news was buzzing up and down the hall. Steven sighed. "The understudy, Millicent Clement—I must call her . . ." he began.

Just then the dressing room door swung open.

Rosacrucia Alba stood framed there, in her green velvet caftan. "Marta, darling, I heard the dreadful news. What can I do to help?"

Marta swung her head up to glare at Rosa. Her mouth opened as if to speak—but of course, no sound came out.

Rosa, clearly undisturbed by Marta's silence, turned to Steven. "I am ready to step into the breach," she announced grandly.

Steven frowned. "Step into the breach? But you already sang a demanding role this afternoon."

Rosa silenced him with a graceful hand. "This audience did not come here to hear an understudy," she declared in rounded tones. "They came to see a star sing *Tosca.* And so they shall."

He paused, adjusted his glasses, then said slowly, "Perhaps it would be best. . . ."

Marta forced out a harsh, grating grunt and began to pull at Steven's arm. He patted her hand soothingly. "Millicent was given no warning; she hasn't warmed up. She's never rehearsed this with us. And, frankly, her voice is second-rate. The audience has already heard one act of superb singing. Millicent would be a letdown for them."

A smile broke across Rosa's face. "I'll need to have the costumes taken in," she reminded Steven. "And I don't know the blocking, though I'm sure I can fake it. David and Eric can help me onstage." Steven and

Rosa walked out of the dressing room together, making plans.

Marta sank her head onto her dressing table, while Greta enveloped her in a consoling hug. Nancy glanced again at the atomizer. She wanted to analyze the liquid inside. But she knew now was not the time. She backed out of the dressing room, closing the door softly behind her.

Once in the hall, Nancy jumped in shock. There stood the reporter from the *Chicago Sentinel*, writing eagerly in her notebook.

Great scoop for her, Nancy thought. Then she stiffened. Had it been just luck for the writer? Or had Rosa set things up this way, to make sure a journalist would witness her saving the day?

Nora Stubbs sidled up next to Nancy. "What a coup for Rosa," she whispered.

Nancy looked at the black-clad composer. Nora was still on Nancy's suspect list. She didn't trust the composer one bit. Still, Nancy reckoned, Nora knew a lot of inside information. There had to be a way to get it out of her—even if she was a suspect.

"What are you, the Phantom of the Opera?" she joked. "You're always here when trouble happens."

Nora fluffed her frizzy black hair. "That's just because I'm always here," she said. "The trouble's a coincidence."

"Is it?" Nancy asked. "It looks to me like Rosa had

everything to gain from Marta's injury."

Nora lowered her voice. "Rosa's been angling to sing *Tosca* for months. It's one of Marta's signature roles, and Rosa wants to show her up. But until now, Steven wouldn't let her. Rosa's only sung *Tosca* in minor productions in Slovenia, and frankly"—Nora cocked an eyebrow—"her voice isn't suited to it. Plus, she's not enough of an actress to convey such a complex character."

Nancy was about to ask more when Steven came back down the hall. "Nancy, give me a hand," he called. He rapped briskly on Marta's door and opened it. "I've called a doctor, Marta. Until then, Miss Drew will help you." He signaled to Nancy to enter the star's dressing room.

Nancy walked in. Marta had taken off her satin dress and long dark wig. With her makeup rubbed off and her frosted hair skimmed back into a bun, she looked pale and shrunken. She reclined on a small hard chaise, hand to her forehead.

Spying the atomizer on the dressing table, Nancy picked it up. "What was in here?" she asked.

Marta shook her head. Greta, wringing her hands, explained, "We always keep mentholated water there, to reduce phlegm and soothe her throat. She usually spritzes her throat after coming offstage."

Nancy unscrewed the bottle top, raised the atomizer to her nose, and took a sniff. A familiar and powerful smell made her reel backward. "Well, there's formaldehyde in here now."

Marta's eyes flew open, terrified.

Nancy summoned up her knowledge of toxic substances. "If we act quickly, we can minimize the damage. The first thing is to drink water—lots of water, to flush it out of her system. Then a glass of milk to neutralize the poison . . ."

In a twinkling, Greta handed a bottle of spring water to Marta. The soprano obediently began to chug it down. "Milk," Greta said uncertainly. "That might be hard to find. Usually singers avoid milk—it coats their throats."

"Try the green room, by the coffeemaker," Nancy said, remembering using milk earlier that day in her coffee.

Greta sprang out the door, surprisingly spry for a woman of her age. Nancy, observing her devotion to Marta, felt assured that the dresser hadn't tampered with Marta's atomizer.

"How could this have happened?" Greta said to Nancy as she came back in with a quart of milk. "Marta sprayed her throat safely from that bottle just before Act One."

"Was this dressing room unattended at any time during the first act?" Nancy asked.

Greta thought carefully as she poured the milk into a glass for Marta. "I was in and out. I went into the green room to make a cup of tea. I also went to Lauren to borrow thread. Tosca's third-act cloak needed mending."

Nancy knew the backstage routine by now. The hallways were often empty during performances. It would be very easy to slip unnoticed in and out of a vacant dressing room. Still, she'd ask around to see if anyone had been seen entering Marta's room.

Only a few minutes later, Steven bustled in with a doctor in tow. Marta sat patiently as the doctor, Dr. Fessenden, looked down her throat with a small flashlight. Nancy explained what she thought had happened. The doctor sniffed the atomizer.

"Formaldehyde all right. Well, Miss Willentz, your throat lining is red and irritated—but there appears to be no muscle damage."

Marta's eyes closed gratefully.

The doctor turned to Nancy. "Lucky for her you were here, young lady. You prescribed just the right thing. If it hadn't been for that milk, she might have absorbed a dangerous amount of the substance."

He faced Marta again. "Keep on drinking the water. Gargle with it, if you can. And do not even attempt to use your voice until noon tomorrow."

"Marta's used to that," Steven said. "The gargling and resting. That's her usual regimen for twelve hours before she sings."

Marta grabbed a pad, scribbled a note, and

handed it to the doctor. He read it and frowned. "Yes, I know you're in *The Marriage of Figaro* tomorrow night. I happen to have tickets, and I looked forward to your performance. But it won't be wise for you to sing so soon after this. I'm sorry."

Marta clasped her hands in a pleading gesture. Her blue eyes beseeched the doctor. Nancy had to hand it to her—the actress didn't need words to express herself.

Dr. Fessenden sighed as he packed up his medical bag. "I'll examine you at noon tomorrow," he told Marta. "I'll make a decision then. That's the best I can do."

Steven sighed. "I hope she'll be ready," he whispered to Nancy as the doctor left. "Who knows what shape Rosa's voice will be in by tomorrow night, after tonight's unscheduled performance. And I've got to salvage whatever I can, if I have any hope of keeping my job."

An usher appeared in the doorway, arms full of flowers and a few gift-wrapped packages. "Miss Willentz, I don't want to disturb you," he said awkwardly, "but these were delivered for you at the intermission."

Marta looked up eagerly. She waved the young man in. He deposited his burden on the small table beside her chaise, and flitted out of the room. "You see, Marta, they don't forget you," Steven said. "You are still beloved."

A brave smile spread over Marta's face as she sifted through her gifts and cards. She lifted up a spangled stuffed butterfly. "From Donald, I bet," Greta gushed. "That darling man. Steadfast as a rock, he is."

Marta nodded, blinking back tears.

Then Nancy saw the diva freeze.

Nancy sprang to her side. Marta wordlessly held up the butterfly.

Twisted around its body was a garnet choker.

Greta gasped. "Marta—it's your stolen necklace!"

10

Another Diva Down

Nancy sprang to Marta's side to look at the necklace. "Was there a note attached?"

Marta shook her head. "Donald never puts a note on his gifts," Greta explained. "If it's a butterfly, we just know it's from him."

Nancy frowned. "But someone else could have sent this, to frame Donald for the theft."

Greta looked skeptical. "Then where is Donald's gift? He always sends something, and it's always a butterfly. This has to be from Donald. Only . . . Where did he get that necklace?"

"Did he know about the burglary?" Steven asked Greta. "Maybe he went out and bought a similar necklace for Marta to replace the one he knew she'd lost."

Greta nodded. "That would be just like Donald. So thoughtful."

Marta had been turning the necklace over in her hands. Looking up, she shook her head. She held it out to Greta, pointing at a small gold medallion hanging from the clasp. Greta studied it and sighed. "The same inscription from Mario. This is the original."

Nancy winced as she saw the two women fingering the necklace. Whatever fingerprints might have been on it were being rubbed away.

Just then a tumult of applause rose from the auditorium. Marta sank back and closed her eyes. As if reading her mind, Steven murmured, "'Vissi d'arte,' Tosca's great show-stopping aria. Sounds like Rosa brought down the house." He turned his face away. Nancy thought that his emotions must be sharply split; he was probably half grateful for Rosa's triumph, and half sharing Marta's pain at being thrust aside.

Suddenly Marta rose from her seat. She strode over to the dressing table and, with one dramatic sweep of her arm, knocked all her makeup paraphernalia to the floor. Greta leaped up and held the distraught singer by her shoulders. "Marta, please . . ."

Marta yanked open her dressing gown, stomped over to the clothes rack, and began raking her fingers through the garments hanging there. "Let's go back to the hotel," Greta suggested. "Before the act ends."

"Great idea," Steven said quickly. "Rest and recuperation, that's the thing. I'll pop out and alert your limousine driver." He ducked out of the dressing room, surely relieved to have an excuse to escape.

"I can't find your cloak, Marta. Maybe it's back at the hotel," Greta fussed. "Here, this will do." She flung a brown overcoat around Marta's shoulders and hurriedly swept together their belongings, including the butterfly and the restored necklace. Nancy bit her lip. She wanted to examine the gift, but it would blow her cover. Until Steven revealed that Nancy was a detective, she had to lie low.

Nancy trailed behind Marta and Rosa as they headed for the stage door. Marta held her chin high, as if refusing to be pitied. The guard muttered some words of sympathy as he swung open the door for the singer.

To Nancy's surprise, there were a dozen people waiting on the sidewalk, even though the opera was not over. Nancy scanned their faces. Donald Tompkins wasn't among them.

The opera buffs crowded around Marta as she emerged. "No autographs," Greta announced, shooing them away as she helped Marta into her limousine.

The fans backed away with sighs of disappointment. Nancy mingled with them. "Anybody see Donald Tompkins?" she asked. "Or did he go inside to watch the second act?"

A young woman looked askance at Nancy. "No way!" she declared. "Donald wouldn't betray Marta like that. Rosacrucia Alba is Willentz's nemesis. All of us have agreed that we won't watch that scheming soprano steal the show."

Nancy was impressed by their dedication to Marta. "So where is Donald now?" Nancy asked.

The fans looked at each other blankly. "We don't know," another fan said. "He was here earlier."

"He's probably too upset by what happened to Willentz," someone else suggested. "He takes this all very personally."

"Where is he staying?" Nancy inquired.

Everyone shrugged as they drifted apart. Nancy got the impression that this odd little band of people were very tight in some respects, but at the same time, they barely knew each other at all.

During Act Three, Nancy took advantage of the stillness backstage to inspect Marta's dressing room. Her search was futile. Anything that belonged to Marta, including the atomizer, had been swept into the case that Greta took away. All that was left was a table full of extravagant flower arrangements, the rack of costumes, and a few standard furnishings. The trash bin held empty water bottles and makeup-smeared cotton balls. There was no evidence that the door lock had been jimmied, or that the tiny window had been opened. Whoever tampered with the atomizer had probably simply walked in.

Discouraged, Nancy headed for a restaurant near the theater. She'd agreed to meet up with George and Bess there. The restaurant's pale pink walls were hung with local artists' work, and jazz music was piped in. Nancy could tell *Tosca* had ended; people were streaming in for after-show drinks. Half an hour later, the cast and crew arrived, chattering and charged up from the performance.

Bess came in, eyes dancing, with Chris, the cute tenor from the chorus. "What, no party tonight?" Nancy asked as they reached her table.

"Of course, but it's back at the hotel, after dinner," Chris replied. "We're starving. We never eat before singing. It makes you sluggish and the food coats the vocal passages."

"I wondered why we were the only ones eating pizza in the green room earlier," Bess said.

Chris nodded. "But I'm so hungry right now I could eat a horse."

"Lucky you found this place," Nancy remarked. "River Heights doesn't have many late-night dining spots—not like they have in New York."

Chris grinned. "If there's a late-night place in town, we singers will find it, believe me!" He waved good-bye and went to join his fellow chorus members at another table.

"Cute guy," George remarked as she joined her

friends. "Looks like you two get all the fun on this case."

"It's been an eventful day," Nancy said. She filled George and Bess in on what had happened.

George listened to Nancy, then reported on her research. She handed her friend a thick file of print-outs from various Internet sites. "Nothing surprising here," she said. "Standard information on Marta, Sean, Rosa, and Nora Stubbs. But did you know Marta was married for about a year, twenty-one years ago? Her husband was named—"

"Mario," Nancy finished. "According to the inscription on the garnet necklace."

George nodded. "Mario Fiorentino. A tenor, much older than Marta. He died seven years ago."

Nancy leafed through the printouts. "Anything on Donald Tompkins?" she asked.

George shook her head. "Nothing. I checked to see where he's staying, but he's not at the Regent Hotel, where most of the company is, or at the River Heights Inn with Rosa, her dresser Paula, and Nora Stubbs. In fact, he's not registered at any hotel in town. I called them all."

Nancy pulled out her pad of paper. "Let's draw a grid," she said. "We have five incidents to investigate: the sandbag and Rosa's burst bodice yesterday, the broken parapet this afternoon, and this evening, the tainted atomizer and the returned necklace." She jotted these on one axis. "Then we'll list all our suspects—Marta, Rosa, Nora, Donald, Jackie—and check their alibis for the time of each incident. . . ."

Bess looked on as Nancy drew her graph. "Trouble is, most of them have no alibi. They were at the theater the whole time."

A moment later the girls saw the restaurant door swing open. The room fell silent, and all eyes turned to the doorway.

Rosa stood poised on the threshold, head thrown back, arms outstretched. An elegant cloak of deep purple wool flowed around her slim figure.

The restaurant burst into wild applause. Chorus members and operagoers alike jumped to their feet.

Nancy met her friends' eyes. "I thought Rosa's diva behavior had made her unpopular."

Bess shrugged. "I guess they'll forgive anyone who sings as beautifully as she did tonight."

From the corner of her eye, Nancy watched Rosa flit among the tables like a honeybee, landing at each one to harvest compliments.

Nancy's concentration was broken by Lauren Sweet. "Nancy," she said, leaning on their table, "you asked me if anybody handled Rosa's costume yesterday. Well, I just remembered something."

Nancy perked up. "What is it?"

"Before the rehearsal," the costumer said, "a

stagehand picked up Rosa's costume. She said she was helping Paula. I was so busy, it didn't occur to me that Rosa wouldn't need her dress for a mere run-through."

George raised her eyebrows. "Which stagehand? Do you remember?"

Lauren nodded. "That girl who's substituting for Jerry Cropper. I forget her name."

"Jackie Ahern," Nancy said. "Thanks for the information, Lauren."

As Lauren left, Nancy turned to face her friends. "Jackie's told a few too many lies. George, did you call those names from her résumé?"

George nodded. "The community college she attended verified that she was enrolled there. And her job contacts in San Francisco checked out okay. But people barely seemed to remember her; she never stayed in any job very long. I couldn't find any address for her; no phone listing or record with the electric company."

"If she lived with roommates, the phone and utilities might have been in their names," Bess said.

Nancy nodded. "That's possible."

"I'll call some roommate-finding agencies tomorrow," George said. "Maybe Jackie used one of them to find a roommate."

"It's a long shot, but it might yield something,"

Nancy agreed. "I hope so. Even if she did lie about being from River Heights, Jackie doesn't strike me as your classic rootless loner."

Suddenly a blare of sirens tore through the air. Nancy jumped to her feet. "Where's Rosa?" she cried. "She was here a minute ago."

Nancy ran out of the café, with George close behind. A trio of police cars, with lights flashing, screeched up to the curb half a block away. Several passersby were already clustered around the mouth of a narrow, dark alley.

Nancy pushed her way through. A few yards into the alley, four police officers knelt beside a figure slumped against the rough brick wall.

Nancy caught a glimpse of purple cloak. Her heart leaped into her throat.

Another siren screamed up behind her. The police officers moved aside to let the emergency medical technicians through. Nancy got her first good look at the victim.

It was Rosa all right. Her face was battered and bruised, her limbs were splayed at awkward angles, and her eyes were shut.

11

Something Borrowed, Someone Blue

Sinking back against the wall to let the EMTs through, Nancy felt miserable. If only she had kept her eyes on Rosa in the café! She'd been so busy considering Rosa as a suspect, she'd forgotten the singer was also a potential victim.

"Hey, Nancy Drew!"

Nancy turned to see a police officer with whom she'd worked before. "Officer Covello!"

"Working on a case?" Covello asked.

Nancy glanced around to make sure no opera company members were within hearing. "Sort of," she hedged.

"You know the victim?" Covello guessed.

Nancy nodded. "Sort of. You need an ID?"

Covello shook her head. "We've got all that. She had her wallet on her."

Nancy raised her eyebrows. "So this wasn't just a mugging?"

"Doesn't look like it." Covello jerked a thumb toward her patrol car. "I'm heading to the hospital to follow up. You girls want a ride?"

"Sure, thanks." Nancy and George climbed into the dark back seat; they'd lost Bess in the commotion, and assumed she was probably with Chris. Nancy pressed the light-up button on her watch to check the time. It was 1:35 A.M. She'd been up since early that morning, and she was exhausted. But she couldn't quit now—not with Rosa Alba being bundled into an ambulance.

"How much should we tell Officer Covello about what's happened in the past couple of days with Marta and Rosa?" George whispered.

"I'd like to get the police involved. This is getting serious," Nancy whispered back. "But it's really Steven Reynolds's decision. Let's call him at the hotel once we get to the hospital, and let him know what happened to Rosa."

Nancy had underestimated the efficiency of the opera grapevine, however. Within moments of the accident, Steven knew about the attack on Rosa. He was already waiting at the River Heights Hospital's emergency room when they arrived, perched on the edge of a vinyl chair. Seeing Nancy and George, he jumped to his feet.

"How is Rosa?" Nancy asked him.

"The doctor's with her now," Steven said. "I must say, I've been at this hospital too much today; first after this afternoon's accident, and now for this." His eyes looked weary and worried at the same time.

"Is Mark Stephens still here?" George asked.

"He went home about an hour ago," Steven said. "His ankle was pretty badly sprained, but once it was taped up, they let him go. Apparently football tryouts are next week, and he'll miss them. Serves him right." He pursed his lips.

"And how's the cellist?" Nancy asked.

"Yvonne?" Steven replied. "She wasn't injured at all, but she was pretty upset. While her eighty-thousand-dollar cello escaped unharmed, her bow was shattered beyond repair."

George shrugged. "So she gets a new bow."

"Not so easy," Steven explained. "You can't just pick up a cello bow at the local music store—not when you play at the level Yvonne Hicks does."

"I've got it!" Nora Stubbs's voice rang out, causing Nancy to wheel around. She was struck by the composer's knack for appearing at times of trouble.

"What's that?" Steven called over to Nora, who was at a nearby bank of pay phones.

"Charlie has a star cellist friend who lives only

forty miles away," Nora announced triumphantly, hanging up a phone. "This guy has no engagements in the next four days. He's willing to lend Yvonne his bow until then; he's heard of her, and he said it'd be an honor."

Steven smiled. "That's perfect! That bowmaker you found in Chicago said he could express mail her new bow in time for Saturday's matinee, right? She can fill in with this borrowed one until then." Impulsively, he threw his arms around Nora. "The opera thanks you."

"Don't thank me; thank the musicians' network," Nora said, pushing back her frizzy black hair. "Me and my friends from music school, we stick together. It wasn't easy, though. Yvonne's picky about her bow, being left-handed and all."

Something stirred in Nancy's brain. *Left-handed.*

Then it all came together in a flash. Of course! The direction of the saw marks on the sabotaged backdrop would have been made by someone sawing with his or her left hand. The severed cords on Rosa's corsets were all on the left side. Their saboteur was most likely left-handed.

Nancy began to search her memory for images of each of her suspects. Had she seen any of them doing anything left-handed?

Her thinking was interrupted by the arrival of a

young doctor in green hospital scrubs. "Mr. Reynolds, you may see Miss Alba now," he said.

"Is she conscious?" Steven asked, his strong voice faltering with concern.

"Oh yes, she's come around," the doctor said. "She has a concussion, but we ran some X-rays and there's no skull fracture. She appears to have been hit from behind by a blunt instrument like a hammer or a wrench." He paused. "Her face is pretty badly bruised. She hasn't seen herself in a mirror yet, so she doesn't know how she looks. I thought I'd let you break it to her."

Steven chuckled grimly. "Knowing how vain Rosa is, she'll be more upset by facial bruises than by a skull fracture."

"I know appearance is important to performers," the doctor noted tactfully. "If it helps, tell her that these are superficial bruises, and they should fade quickly. Her skin is hardly cut anywhere. Whatever she was hit with had no sharp edges."

The attacker obviously meant to scare Rosa but not to kill her, Nancy thought after Steven and Nora left to visit Rosa. *And it wasn't a robbery. Who would do this?*

"If her face is bruised, she'll have to cancel a performance or two," George said. "For Rosa, that would be a major setback."

"Not to mention a setback for the American

Grand Opera Company," Nancy said. "One star was knocked out of *Tosca* this evening, and now the other one might be out of commission for a while. If Marta's throat hasn't healed by noon tomorrow, *Figaro* won't have any name singers."

"Sean Torrance," George reminded her, stifling an early morning yawn.

"Sean isn't the caliber of singer that people buy tickets to see," Nancy said. "It sure looks as if somebody's trying to hurt the company as a whole."

George considered this. "Who would have a grudge against the company?" She paused a moment before suggesting a name. "Nora Stubbs?"

Nancy hesitated. "Earlier in the day, I would have said so. But you saw her just now; Nora was scrambling to help that cellist get the bow she needed. Saboteurs don't generally turn around and help whomever they're sabotaging."

"Unless she wants to look like a hero," George argued. "Now that Steven owes her a favor, he might be more likely to produce her new opera."

Suddenly the emergency room's automatic doors cranked open. Nancy and George saw none other than Marta Willentz, hair piled high, arms cradling a massive bouquet. Greta scurried over to the front desk to ask directions to Rosa's room. Beside Marta stood a skinny young man in an olive-green velour track suit—Donald Tompkins.

Marta had managed to regain her majestic manner. Her commanding gaze swept the waiting room as Greta talked to the nurses.

Greta trotted back to Marta and whispered something in her ear. With a flourish, Marta pulled out a tiny notepad with a silver pen attached and scribbled a response to Greta's question. Nancy noted that Marta was right-handed.

"Don't tell me she's here to console Rosa," George whispered in disbelief. "She probably took that bouquet from the stash in her own dressing room! There's a public relations stunt if I ever saw one. And who's that skinny guy with her?"

"The mysterious Donald Tompkins," Nancy whispered back, watching him to see if he did anything left-handed.

As the diva and her entourage passed, Marta spotted Nancy. She drew to a halt, lowered her eyelids, and laid a hand lightly on Nancy's wrist. "We rushed over as soon as we heard about Rosa," Greta spoke for Marta. "What an awful accident, especially after what happened to Marta earlier."

Marta tore a page off of her notepad and handed it to Nancy. In a curlicued scrawl, she had written, *My heart bleeds for my sister in distress. I must be with her. Come with us.*

"I guess she needs an audience for this scene," George whispered in Nancy's ear as they followed

Marta down the bare white corridor.

Rosa Alba's frail figure lay wrapped in the white sheets on her hospital bed. Her battered face was turned away from the door. Steven sat on a chair next to her bed, holding her limp hand.

"Marta!" Nora said in surprise, shooting up from the chair near the door.

Marta cocked her head sorrowfully and laid her hand briefly against Nora's cheek. Then, drawing a deep breath, she turned toward Rosa.

Nancy was amazed to see the joyful look that flooded onto Rosa's bruised and swollen face as she recognized her visitor. "Marta!" she cried out. "You came to see me?"

Marta swept over to the bed. She closed her eyes, crossed her arms over her chest, and made a deep curtsy. Rising, she reached out and grasped both of Rosa's hands in her own.

Tears began to flood Rosa's dark eyes. "You don't know how much this means to me, Marta," she began to babble. "This late at night—and after what happened earlier—"

Donald popped up beside Marta and set the bouquet on Rosa's bedside table. "Now you, too, know what it means to be viciously attacked," he said in his whiny voice. "You and Marta have this in common now."

Marta released Rosa's hands and groped for her

notepad. Rosa brushed away the tears that were beginning to stream down her damaged cheeks.

Steven had risen to his feet. "You two have always had more in common than you realize," he declared. "What better time could there be for you both to bury thc hatchet?"

Marta looked up at Steven. Then her eyes focused on something behind him.

She froze, then slowly raised her hand, index finger trembling. She pointed to the coatrack, where the purple cloak Rosa had been wearing that evening hung.

A tiny shriek escaped from Greta. "Where did that cape come from?" she exclaimed. "It's Marta's!"

12

Soprano Switch

Nancy jumped to the logical conclusion. *If Rosa was wearing Marta's cloak when she was attacked from behind, then her attacker might have thought she was Marta.* She suppressed a shiver.

It only took a moment for everyone else in the hospital room to realize the same thing. Looking at Marta's stricken face, Nancy guessed that the older soprano was convinced this second attack was meant for her. Given what had happened to her earlier, it was a pretty chilling thought.

Marta's mouth flew open and she made a tiny, strangled noise. Donald and Greta grabbed her by either arm. "You mustn't speak!" Greta cried out.

"Silence, silence," Donald urged Marta. "You know what the doctor said."

Marta's face crumpled in a complicated mix of fear, anger, and frustration. Suddenly turning on her heel, she stormed out of the room with Greta and Donald right behind her.

Rosa, in the hospital bed, threw up her hands. "Why is it always about her?" she fumed. "I'm the one who was hurt. Why does it matter if I was wearing her ridiculous cloak?" She stumbled over the last word.

Steven patiently took her hand. "Of course, Rosa, darling. But why *did* you have it on? Everybody in the company knows that cloak belongs to Marta. She wears it everywhere. You can't tell me you didn't know it was hers."

Rosa thrust out her jaw. "It was Sara Tucci's idea," she replied in a low, sullen voice. "She brought it to me during the second intermission. She said if I was going to take over Marta's role, I might as well take over her cloak."

Steven sighed. "And then I bet she pointed it out to that Chicago reporter. Another of Sara's less-than-brilliant ideas. And this time, the idea backfired."

"What do you mean?" Rosa's voice began to rise. "Why do you assume the attacker was after Marta? He was after me, me, me!"

"Now, Rosa, don't get agitated," Steven said anxiously. "You've been through a lot. Let's ask the nurse for a sedative." He threw Nancy a pleading look. She and George slipped out the door to go find a nurse.

"Even *now,* Rosa won't yield the spotlight to Marta," George said to Nancy in the hall.

"She does have a point, though" Nancy said. "We can't be certain the attacker was after Marta. But one good thing has come of this: Steven has to let the police investigate now. Maybe that will help us get to the bottom of this."

The next morning, after being tipped off by Nancy and Steven, the police descended on the River Heights Theater. After taking over Steven's office, two detectives began calling in each member of the company for questioning.

"Nancy, aren't you sitting in on the interviews?" Steven asked as he saw Nancy pouring a cup of coffee in the green room. The long low-ceilinged room wasn't exactly the coziest place to relax, with its windowless painted-brick walls and scuffed blue plastic furniture. Still, it was a communal spot that the singers and crew were drawn to.

Nancy shook her head. Glancing around to make sure no one overheard her, she said, "The detectives have agreed to play the taped interviews for me later. I don't want to blow my cover yet. It's often the case if someone's hiding something from the police, they spill the truth to somebody else after they're questioned. I intend to hang around all day, offering a sympathetic ear to my suspects."

Steven smiled wanly. "I see you know what you're doing." He gulped. "I'd better call the board of directors. They've probably read about yesterday afternoon's accident, but Rosa's attack happened too late to be in the papers yet. Maybe I can perform a little damage control—and possibly save my job." He hurried away.

Lauren stepped into the green room, looking shaken. Nancy offered her a cup of coffee. "Thanks, Nancy," Lauren said, taking the cup and sinking into a chair. "I hate feeling like I'm suspected of something and put under the hot lights."

Nancy looked surprised. "Suspected? Surely they don't think you did anything. You were inside the restaurant when Rosa was attacked. I saw you there myself. Detectives all have suspicious minds—it's part of their job," Nancy consoled Lauren. "I wouldn't think much of it. Is Paula with them now?"

Lauren nodded. "I hope they don't give her a rough time. She doesn't deserve it."

Nancy was still in the green room, leafing through a magazine, when Paula emerged from the office. She looked distressed. As soon as she saw Nancy tears swam into her eyes. "They accused *me!*" she burst out. "They hinted that I stayed late at the theater only so I could sneak out and attack Rosa." Her lip quivered as she took the cup of coffee Nancy handed her.

"If they knew anything about the theater, they'd

know that costume people are always the last to leave," Nancy said.

Paula nodded. "But I'm afraid they'll ask the other members of the company if I might have a grudge against Rosa. And everybody will remember Rosa scolding me for something or other. People don't understand; a diva has to vent her stress on somebody. That's one of the reasons she needs her dresser. The dresser *always* understands."

"Of course. Were you with Rosa when she left the theater last night?" Nancy asked.

Paula nodded. "I walked her to the stage door. I offered to go with her, but she wanted to make her entrance at the restaurant alone. She looked so lovely in that purple cape. . . ."

Nancy cocked her head. "She knew it was Marta's cape, didn't she? Why did she borrow it?"

"Sara Tucci brought it to her," Paula said. "Then Sara walked by with that reporter, to make sure she saw Rosa wearing it. Rosa loved the symbolism of it." She wiped away a tear. "To think that wearing that cape led her to such danger!"

Nancy noted that the backstage grapevine, at work once again, had already decided the attack was meant for Marta, not Rosa. The cape had convinced the members of the company; they weren't willing to allow that it might be just a coincidence that Rosa had been wearing Marta's cape.

Paula took another sip of coffee. "Well, I'd better pull myself together. I promised Rosa I'd be at the hospital by noon, when visiting hours start. Steven asked me to come here first to talk to the police, but Rosa needs me now."

Bess soon arrived in the green room, waving a newspaper. "I just got the *Chicago Sentinel.* The story about Rosa made the front page."

Nancy winced. "That reporter was here to write a feature story, and she ended up getting late-breaking gossip. Let's see how bad it is." The girls spread out the newspaper on a coffee table by the long sofa.

> *RIVER HEIGHTS—It's every understudy's dream. A sudden ailment befalls the superstar in midshow. The cry goes out for someone to step into her role. Presto! A star is born.*
>
> *But for Slovenian soprano Rosacrucia Alba, her lucky break took a nasty turn last night.*
>
> *Alba's brilliant stand-in performance as Tosca in the American Grand Opera's touring production proved she was ready to assume the mantle of Marta Willentz, one of opera's greatest stars. But when Alba assumed the mantle* literally*—borrowing a purple cloak from the ailing Willentz's dressing room and*

walking into the cool night—a mysterious attacker added a tragic last act to the singer's bout of triumph.

"Is that the *Sentinel* article?" Steven asked as he walked in. "Someone on the board of directors already read it. They're furious." He sighed. "And that's nothing compared to how furious Rosa will be to see herself called Marta's understudy."

He crossed over to the company bulletin board and tacked up a sheet of paper. "When people come in, make sure they read this. It's a last-minute change to the schedule. Since Rosa's too ill to appear in *Figaro* this evening, we're going to perform *Tosca* again. The doctor has just examined Marta and says she's healed enough to sing. Hopefully, Rosa will feel up to doing *Figaro* by Saturday afternoon."

Just then George popped her head in the door. "Nancy, got a minute?" she asked, nearly breathless with excitement.

The three friends huddled together in the corner. "What did you learn, George?" Nancy asked.

"I had a lucky break. One roommate agency in San Francisco had Jackie in its files," George said. "I pretended Jackie was applying to be my roommate and I wanted to check her references. They connected me with Jackie's old roommate, Danielle Finch. She was a gold mine of information."

"Yeah?" Nancy said, excited.

"For one thing," George reported, "she says Jackie was born overseas and lived all over Europe as a kid. Her parents were in the U.S. Army. Or maybe I should say her *adoptive* parents. After they moved back to the States, Jackie bounced from college to college, never graduating, trying to figure herself out. By the time she lived with Danielle, she had a new mission: to find her birth mother."

Bess whistled. "That can be hard—especially if the birth mother doesn't want to be found."

George nodded. "Even harder since she was adopted in Europe, where the record-keeping isn't uniform. And, by then, both her adoptive parents had died, so they couldn't give her any facts about her birth parents. But Jackie persisted. She finally tracked the woman down."

"Did her mom agree to meet her?" Bess asked.

"Danielle's not sure what happened. Jackie was very secretive about it," George said. "But it seemed Jackie anticipated that her mother would rebuff her, so she decided to take her by surprise. One day, six months ago, she asked Danielle to go with her to see her birth mother for the first time." George paused. "They went to the San Francisco Opera House."

Nancy's mind raced ahead. "Who?" she began asking.

George met her eyes. "I went online to check what opera was being performed that day. It was *Madame Butterfly*."

Nancy closed her eyes, remembering Donald's stream of butterfly gifts. Of course—Marta's signature role.

"And who was singing the lead that day?" George finished her tale. "None other than Marta Willentz."

Nancy leaned toward George intently. "Was that who Jackie went to see?"

George sat back in her chair and sighed. "Danielle has no idea. Jackie asked her to wait outside while Jackie went into the opera house. Fifteen minutes later Jackie came storming out, refusing to talk about it. Danielle figured Jackie would eventually tell her, but she never did. A few weeks later, Jackie suddenly announced she was leaving San Francisco. She left a lot of stuff in the apartment for Danielle to keep."

Just then Nancy's neck got a prickly feeling, as if someone were close behind her. She turned to see Sean Torrance standing there, a grief-stricken look on his face. "You can't let Marta know," he croaked.

"Know what?" Nancy asked, wondering how much of the conversation Sean had overheard.

"That Jackie Ahern is her daughter," Sean replied.

13

The Lost Girl

"You knew all along that Marta was Jackie's mother?" Nancy gasped.

Sean hung his head down and dropped into a chair beside Bess. "Not until this minute. But I knew there was a daughter somewhere. . . ."

"Go on," Nancy coaxed in a low voice.

Sean leaned his head wearily on one hand. "That chapter of Marta's life is over. She was so young when she got involved with Mario Fiorentino. She was a rising star."

"Like Rosa, today?" Nancy couldn't help saying.

Sean winced, but he nodded. "Mario was much older; he was in the last days of his career. And he was never that much of a star. They got married, but the marriage soon fell apart. He couldn't handle

Marta's growing success. Professional jealousy can be a very ugly thing."

"So we've noticed," George commented.

"Marta was the one who filed for divorce," Sean continued. "Mario flew into a rage and left her stranded in Vienna. By the time she learned she was going to have a baby, she knew their marriage was over. She never even told him she was pregnant with their child."

Bess gasped. "He never knew?"

Sean shook his head. "Marta withdrew from the stage for six or seven months. Rumors swirled around, of course; some people said she'd had a nervous breakdown. The whole time, she was in seclusion in Switzerland, waiting to give birth. She gave the baby up for adoption right after it was born, and made a triumphant return to the stage. She never told anyone the truth."

"Except you," Nancy said.

"Not even me." Sean forced out a small, wry smile. "All this happened long before I knew her. I pieced together the story over the years. She doesn't even know I know."

"What a terrible secret for Marta to carry around for so long," Bess said sympathetically.

"This is why she is a great tragic actress," Sean declared dramatically. "She knows sorrow. She lives for her art—and she has paid the price!"

George couldn't help rolling her eyes when Sean wasn't looking. "Well, now we know why Jackie was upset after meeting Marta in San Francisco," she said. "Marta must not have welcomed her when she showed up after all those years."

Sean gave George a look of concern. "But I told you—Marta doesn't know."

"But Jackie went to meet her . . ."

"Did your research show you who else was singing in *Madame Butterfly* that day? In the role of Sharpless?" Sean narrowed his eyes. "It was me."

"You were there too?" Nancy said. An uneasy sensation rocked her stomach.

"Yes. I was backstage when that girl showed up," Sean said. "She wanted to accost Marta between acts—before Marta had to go on and sing *Un bel di*. One of the greatest arias ever written! And no one sings it like Marta can."

Sean shifted in his seat. "San Francisco is a very big opera city," he continued, his voice growing more powerful. "There were several major critics in the audience. At that stage in her career, every performance was critical. How could I let that child ruin it for her?"

Nancy gasped. "So you just . . . sent Jackie away?"

Sean nodded. "But don't you see? Her appearing would have done nothing other than disrupt Marta's career. Marta didn't need a daughter hanging around. Today, she fights every day to deny her age. What would having a grown daughter do to her public image?"

Nancy swallowed hard, but there was a giant lump in her throat that just wouldn't go away. Nancy had been only three when her mother died. If she'd ever had a chance to see her own mother again, and a meddling stranger had prevented her—she began to seethe, just thinking of it.

"Believe me," Sean added in a pleading tone, "it took Marta years to get over the pain of abandoning her child. What point is there in opening the wound?" He rose to his feet. "Just promise me one thing: Don't let Marta know."

Nancy's eyes flashed. "How can I keep such information from Marta? She's Jackie's mother; she has a right to know. And it's not your business to decide their fate."

George touched Nancy lightly on the arm and gave her a steadying look. Nancy took a deep breath. George was right. She was losing her focus. She was here to solve a mystery, not to sort out people's complicated lives.

"Let me get this straight," George took over. "You knew Jackie was here, working with the stage crew, and you never told anyone who she was?"

Sean sighed. "I didn't recognize her, I swear. She looks so different now. She cut her hair short, she bleached it . . . besides, when I saw her six months ago, I only spoke to her for a minute."

"I'm going to have to inform the police," Nancy said crisply. "Jackie is one of our—I mean, *their* chief suspects. She was near the sandbag when it fell; she took Rosa's bodice to her dressing room on Tuesday; she was adjusting the parapet before it broke Wednesday afternoon. The police need to know that there's a material connection between her and one of the victims."

"All right, but let me break the news to Marta," Sean pleaded, slowly stepping away. "It's better if it comes from a close friend. I'll choose the right moment, and the right words."

Nancy shrugged, still distrusting the baritone. "I guess that'll be okay," she said warily.

Once Sean was out of earshot, George and Bess leaned close to Nancy. "Nan, do you really think Jackie is our culprit?" Bess whispered.

Nancy frowned. "Why? Just because she came here to be close to her birth mother? That doesn't prove that she wants to hurt Marta. And it certainly doesn't give her a motive to hurt Rosa." She paused for a moment. "But yes, I guess it does make Jackie look a lot more suspicious. Let's go find her and make sure she talks to the police."

The girls got up and began to hunt through all the nooks and crannies of the old theater. Jackie Ahern didn't appear to be anywhere.

"Mike, have you seen Jackie?" Nancy called out to Mike Cordasco, who was nailing together a new parapet in the set shop.

Mike looked up and pushed his baseball cap back. "Huh? Jackie? No, she hasn't clocked in yet. She was supposed to be here by nine A.M. too. If you see her, give her a warning: Doug's ready to skin her alive." He winked, but he didn't seem to be really joking.

Nancy's stomach fluttered. Was Jackie absent because the police were grilling everyone at the theater today?

"I'm not surprised if she's playing hookey today," another stagehand at the worktable grumbled. "She's always sneaking off when she should be here working."

"That's not entirely true," Mike said. "She was here late last night, wasn't she? She struck the set with the rest of us. She even offered to finish the prop inventory so the rest of you bozos could go back to the hotel."

"She was here?" Nancy said. Maybe Jackie *did* have an alibi for last night. "What time?"

The stagehands looked vaguely at each other. "I left around one o'clock, and she was still here then," one said. "At least, I think it was one. It was ten after one when I got to my hotel room—I know that for certain."

Nancy slumped a little. The police had put the

time of Rosa's attack at one fifteen A.M. If Jackie was here at one, she could easily have scooted across the street and attacked Rosa by one fifteen.

"I saw her in the prop room later," another hand mentioned.

"When was that?" Nancy asked hopefully.

"Two o'clock," he said firmly. "I remember that the hour alarm on my wrist watch beeped when I walked past the prop room, and it gave her a scare. You know, you get kinda jumpy when you're working after hours all alone in a big, deserted building like this."

Nancy nodded. Unfortunately, she could think of other reasons why Jackie might have been jumpy at two o'clock last night.

"So no one saw Jackie between one and two this morning?" Nancy checked one last time.

The men shrugged and shook their heads.

"Thanks. Oh, and one more thing," Nancy asked, somewhat reluctantly. "Did you ever happen to notice whether Jackie is left-handed?"

"Jackie? Why, as a matter of fact, she is," Mike said, scratching his head. "I noticed it the other day, when we were side by side, hammering down a flat. Our elbows kept crashing, till we figured out that we needed to switch places."

"Just curious," Nancy said with a sigh. "Thanks, guys."

"Let's go to Steven's office and get Jackie's résumé," Nancy suggested to George and Bess as they left the set shop. "Maybe Jackie's at home, sick. We'll call her and find out."

The police detectives were in the middle of questioning David Landers when Nancy knocked on the door to Steven's office. The lead detective, Ronald Zhang, knew Nancy from a few previous cases with which she had helped. Without pausing in his interview, he nodded permission for Nancy to rummage around the office. She tucked the personnel file under her arm and slipped back out into the hall.

"Here's her home number," Nancy said, reading Jackie's résumé. "It's 555-3216. Have you got your cell phone with you, George?"

"Right here." George whipped out her tiny cellular phone and punched in the numbers. She then handed Nancy her phone.

Nancy listened to the tinny bleeps of the phone ringing. *Come on, Jackie, be there,* she said to herself.

The line clicked and a man's voice came on. "Hello?"

"Jackie Ahern, please," Nancy said.

"Who?"

Nancy hesitated. "Jackie Ahern?"

"No one here by that name," the man growled.

"Did I dial 555-3216?" Nancy asked quickly before the man could hang up. Bess looked down at the résumé and nodded to verify that this was indeed the right number.

"That's this number," the man grumbled. "And there's no Jackie Ahern here. I've never heard of anybody by that name. So good-bye." The line went dead.

Nancy hung up with a sinking heart. There it was: another lie on Jackie's résumé.

Even worse, Nancy realized, was that she had no idea now how to find Jackie Ahern.

14

Butterfly Must Die

Time to face facts, Nancy told herself sternly. Nancy finally had to admit that the probability was high that Jackie was the culprit she sought.

Nancy turned abruptly to the uniformed policeman standing guard outside the interview room. "There's a very important suspect who hasn't come in for questioning. I have an address for her here. Could you have someone go pick her up? I'm pretty sure she has something against Marta Willentz."

The officer looked confused. "But I thought we were here to investigate the attack on Rosacrucia Alba. What does Marta Willentz have to do with it?"

Detective Zhang stuck his head out of the office door. He must have overheard some of the conversation. "Don't worry, Turnbull. Like I told you before,

Miss Drew is a crucial part of this investigation. If she asks you to check out something, check it out. All right?"

It only took a few moments for the police to mobilize in the search for Jackie Ahern. A patrol car soon radioed in to Detective Zhang, reporting that the address from Jackie's résumé didn't even exist. Meanwhile, Nancy huddled with the detectives in Steven's office, outlining her reasons for suspecting Jackie. She also gave them a full physical description of the missing stagehand. An A.P.B.—all points bulletin—was immediately sent out.

Next, Nancy put in a call to River Heights police headquarters, to an officer she knew in the computer department. "Officer Devine?" Nancy said, once her friend was on the line. "This afternoon I want to send you a six month travel itinerary for one of the victims in this opera case we're working on. Would it be possible for you to run a cross-check with passenger lists from train, bus, airline, and car rental companies, looking for the name Jackie Ahern, or maybe Jacqueline Ahern? That's A-H-E-R-N. See how many matches you get. If we can tie Miss Ahern's travels to Marta Willentz's, we may have some proof that she conspired to hurt Miss Willentz."

"Sure thing, Nancy," Officer Devine replied. "That sort of thing usually takes a few hours, but there's a good chance we'll turn something up."

Nancy hung up the phone, grateful for having the police department's assistance at last. "I've sat around too long on this case, watching while other people got hurt," she declared to George and Bess, fishing a sandwich out of the bag her friends had brought from a nearby deli. "It's time for action. We'll find Steven, and get the phone number of Marta's agent in New York. She'd be able to e-mail a list of Marta's recent appearances to Officer Devine."

Nancy strode down the brick hall. George and Bess jogged behind her, hurrying to keep up. "So you're sure now that Jackie is the one behind the accidents?" Bess asked.

Nancy blew out a frustrated breath. "Am I sure? No. Unfortunately, we don't have any hard evidence linking her to any of the incidents. No fingerprints, no eye witnesses, no incriminating objects." Suddenly she stopped speaking and motioned for her friends to duck into an alcove where they wouldn't be noticed.

"On the other hand," Nancy went on in a terse low voice, "we do seem to have a motive, and some strong circumstantial links." She ticked the points off on her fingers. "Jackie was on the catwalk when the sandbag fell. Jackie picked up Rosa's costume from the wardrobe shop before the rehearsal when the bodice split open. And Jackie was seen messing around with the parapet shortly before Mark Stephens crashed through it."

"Wait, Nancy. You're always telling us not to jump to conclusions," George pointed out, crossing her arms "But aren't you jumping to a conclusion right now?"

Nancy frowned. "What do you mean?"

"What if all the incidents weren't caused by the same person?" George said. "Remember, we speculated that one person would've had a hard time slashing Paula Konstance's tires and still returning here in time to cut Rosa's bodice strings. And another thing: Jackie wasn't even with the company last week when the scenery fell on that other stagehand."

Unwrapping her sandwich, Nancy considered this last fact. "That's true. But Jackie might have snuck into the theater in Preston City to take care of that. Once we get that police computer search going, it may very well show that Jackie was in Preston City last week."

"Even so," Bess pitched in, "Jackie might have an alibi for the time when Marta's throat spray was tampered with, or when Rosa was attacked. We won't find that out until she's questioned by the police. And if you're talking about motive, what motive does Jackie have to hurt Rosa? I thought it was her mother she was angry with."

Nancy chewed her sandwich thoughtfully. "If you

think about it, most of the attacks were against Marta. The toppling scenery last week? That was in *Tosca,* an opera that Rosa doesn't appear in. The sandbag? Rosa just *happened* to be standing next to Marta when it fell. The throat spray was clearly an attack on Marta. And the attack in the alley—Rosa was wearing Marta's cape, wasn't she?"

"Plus it was Marta's jewelry that was stolen earlier," George added.

Bess sighed. "Steven *did* say that most of it was jewelry that was given to Marta long ago by her husband; in other words, Jackie's father. That might be reason enough for Jackie to steal the jewelry."

Nancy tapped a finger against one cheek. "But then why would she have returned that necklace yesterday, clasped around the stuffed butterfly?"

Bess shrugged. "I don't know. As a warning, maybe?"

"A warning about what?" Nancy pondered. "I still can't figure out what Jackie could hope to achieve with all this, anyway."

The three girls strolled silently back into the main hall, each one busy with her own thoughts. Nothing about this case was cut-and-dry, Nancy realized. If Jackie was the culprit, she hadn't necessarily succeeded by being a clever or skillful criminal. It was just that her crimes were so petty—and so random—that no one could predict them. In the chaos of the busy opera production, she had been able to slip beneath the radar.

But the crimes might not remain petty, Nancy thought uneasily. So far, each one had been worse than the one before. And who knew what would come next?

Then a glimpse of a figure down the corridor caught Nancy's attention. "There's Greta," she said. "That must mean Marta's in the theater building somewhere."

"Not a surprise," Bess said. "The doctor gave her a clean bill of health, and she's due to sing tonight. It's her chance to reassert herself in the role of Tosca, after all. If I were her, I'd be here, preparing for my performance."

"I wonder if she's been interviewed by Detective Zhang yet," Nancy said, half to herself. "Even more importantly, I wonder if Sean has had a chance to talk to her yet. He promised he would."

Bess touched Nancy's shoulder. "You promised, too, Nancy—you promised you'd let him be the one to tell her about Jackie," she reminded her friend. "It's only fair."

Nancy paused. "Well, she's waited twenty years to meet her daughter. I guess a couple more hours won't hurt. But somehow I doubt Sean has the courage to do it. And if Marta's in danger . . ." Her voice trailed off.

Nancy stuffed her half-uneaten sandwich into the nearest trash bin. She moved toward Marta's dressing room like a moth drawn to a flame. Bess and George hesitantly followed her.

Nancy reached the half-open doorway of the dressing room and peered in. Neither Greta nor Marta seemed to be there. Nancy cautiously pushed the door open wider, and took a step inside.

Marta's personal belongings were strewn around the room. Nancy's eye fell on Donald's stuffed butterfly from yesterday, perched on the dressing table. The garnet necklace was still twisted around its waist.

Nancy gasped.

Thrust into the butterfly's abdomen was a slender silver dagger. A square of white paper hung on the dagger with the ominous words: BUTTERFLY MUST DIE.

15

The Last Act Looms

Nancy heard Bess suck in her breath. "Nancy, you didn't tell us about that nasty message," she said in a shaky voice.

"That's because it wasn't there before," Nancy replied. "George, go find Zhang and let him take a look at this. Bess, stay here and guard this room. Don't let anybody touch that butterfly. We finally have a chance to take some fingerprints in this case."

Nancy ran off to find the security guard who'd been posted outside the stage door since six A.M. She knew he'd been ordered not to let in anyone who wasn't part of the company, and to make everyone who did enter sign a log. Nancy scanned the log; she didn't find Jackie's name. *I guess we already knew she wasn't here,* Nancy thought. *But if she wasn't here, she couldn't have left that note.*

But then who did?

Reentering the building, Nancy searched for Steven. She found him in the room where the musicians kept their gear. He and the cellist, Yvonne Hicks, were inspecting the bow she'd borrowed from Nora's friend's friend.

The pleased smile on Steven's face disappeared when Nancy told him about the note. He handed the bow back to Yvonne and followed Nancy back to Marta's dressing room. "Has Greta seen this note?" he asked as they hurried down the brick hall. "I know she's here somewhere."

"She wasn't in the room," Nancy said.

But Greta was in there now, frantically pacing. When Nancy walked in, Greta grabbed her arm. "Miss Drew, thank goodness," the dresser said. "Where did this horrid thing come from?"

"I'm wondering the same thing," Nancy said.

"I never saw it before," Greta said. "I brought in all of Marta's personal belongings this afternoon. You see, she leaves nothing in the dressing room overnight anymore—not since the burglary. I set that butterfly on the dressing table, then I went to the police for questioning. I swear that note wasn't there when I left."

"Where was the butterfly last night?" Nancy asked Greta.

"In my hotel room," Greta explained. "The very sight of it upset Marta, but I couldn't throw it out; that would hurt Donald's feelings. And I knew Marta would eventually want the necklace back."

"Do you recognize this handwriting?" Nancy asked, pointing to the red scrawl on the note.

Greta stepped closer to peer at it. "No," she said. "But I *do* recognize that knife."

Nancy raised her eyebrows. "You do?"

"That's another item that was stolen from Marta," Greta said. "It's a stage prop from *Madame Butterfly*. The Emperor of Japan himself presented this one to Marta. It's the hara-kiri knife Butterfly uses to kill herself in the third act."

Nancy was startled. "Butterfly kills herself?"

"Of course," Greta said. "Her American husband, Pinkerton, has abandoned her, leaving her in Japan with her little boy. At the end, he returns, but only to take the boy away from her. It's a very tragic opera."

No wonder Marta could sing it with such passion, Nancy realized. She'd been in the same position as Butterfly once in her life. Only, *she'd* made the decision to give away her child.

"Where is Marta now?" Steven asked.

Greta looked confused. "I'm not sure. After Dr. Fessenden examined her at the hotel, I told her she had to come to the theater, to meet the police. That's what you said when you called this morning,

Steven. But she wouldn't come with me. She said she needed time alone at the hotel to prepare for tonight's performance." Greta's eyes narrowed. "Last night was so traumatic for her. You're lucky she agreed to try to sing at all. It's only because she's such a trouper."

"Please," Steven retorted. "Wild horses couldn't keep Marta away from that stage tonight; we both know that. This is her chance to prove herself again." He whipped out his cell phone. "What's the number of your hotel?"

Greta gave him the number and Steven dialed. "Hello? Yes, I'd like to speak to one of your guests. Maria Fiorentino." He winked at Nancy. "Marta's alias on the road," he whispered. "So outsiders don't find her hotel room."

Steven listened for a moment, then frowned. "No answer? But I was told she was in her room. Could you ask the doormen if she left the hotel?"

Nancy twisted her hands anxiously inside her sweatshirt sleeves. Could Marta have been so foolish as to leave the hotel unescorted?

"And what time was that? Thank you." Steven ended the call and looked up grimly. "Marta left in a taxi about an hour ago."

Nancy blew out a tense breath. "An hour ago? But the hotel's only a couple of blocks from the theater." She turned to Greta. "Did she have any appointment, or any special errand to do today?"

Greta shook her head. "She led me to believe she was just resting at the hotel."

"We'd better radio the police patrol cars to find her," Nancy decided. "Meanwhile, George, explain to Steven about getting Marta's itinerary sent to Officer Devine. I'm going to find Detective Zhang to tell him what's happened." She rushed out of the dressing room and went to talk to Detective Zhang.

Half an hour later, as she left Zhang's office, Nancy noticed a flurry of activity near the stage door that led outside. She swivelled to see Marta Willentz marching grandly through the door, beaming and nodding graciously to everyone in sight. Nancy sighed with relief. Wherever Marta had gone, at least she was here safely now.

Then, from the corner of her eye, Nancy saw Donald, hovering near Marta's dressing room. He clutched a needlepointed cushion with a butterfly design on it to his chest.

Nancy frowned. How had Tompkins gotten in? She broke into a jog, heading toward him. "Hey!" she called out.

A terrified look crossed Donald's face. He dropped the cushion, turned on his heels, and dashed away.

Nancy was a fast runner, but Donald had a decent head start, and the narrow hallways in the back of the theater offered many places to hide. Nancy soon accepted that she'd lost him. She ran back to question the stage door guard. "I saw an outsider in here: a young guy with a brown goatee, in a gray tweed jacket," she said.

"You mean Donald?" the guard said.

Nancy hesitated. "Actually, yes. He's not an authorized member of the company."

The guard shrugged. "Everybody knows Donald. I figured the rule didn't apply to him."

Frustrated, Nancy bit her lip. She was in no position to reprimand the guard. She headed back to Marta's dressing room. At this point, protecting Marta was of paramount importance.

As she entered the room she saw that someone—probably the police—had removed the butterfly with its bloody message. That was good; Marta didn't need to be upset by it. But in its place on the dressing room table sat the needlepoint pillow Donald had brought.

"Donald's gift for tonight," Greta's voice came from behind the door. Nancy turned to see Greta sitting on the chaise, brushing out the long dark wig Marta would wear as Tosca.

Nancy picked up the cushion. "Lovely. But what's this hard part?" Turning it over, she found a brooch pinned on the cushion's back side.

Greta hurried over to examine it with her. She gasped. "Another of Marta's missing things! See here?" She pointed to the pair of entwined initials painted on the brooch's enameled face. "M. W. and M. F.: Marta Willentz and Mario Fiorentino."

Nancy cleared her throat. "The police really ought to see this. Can I take it?"

Greta nodded, eyes round with fear.

Preoccupied with the investigation, Nancy stumbled blankly through her walk-on part in the first act of *Tosca* that night. But she did notice how beautifully Marta was singing. The diva blithely poured out her soul in song, as if the previous twenty-four hours hadn't happened.

Watching her, however, Nancy couldn't help but also see the selfish young singer who had abandoned her own daughter twenty years ago. In a way, it spoiled the whole effect.

After the intermission, Nancy wandered into the costume shop to hang up her nun's habit. Lauren looked up and waved. "Guess what?" she bubbled. "Donald was just in here to collect his costume. He's going to have the thrill of his life tonight."

Nancy tensed up. "What's that?"

"He's going onstage alongside Marta! He's playing one of the soldiers in the firing squad scene. Apparently they needed another extra because that guy had gotten hurt yesterday."

"Who authorized that Donald should replace him?" Nancy asked warily.

Lauren shrugged. "Steven, I guess. Isn't it cool?"

Nancy nodded, but as she left the costume shop, she felt uneasy. Even though most clues pointed to Jackie as the criminal at this point, Nancy wasn't ready to cross Donald off her suspect list.

As she ducked into the green room she saw George and Bess lounging on the sofa. With a finger, she motioned for them to follow her. They hopped to their feet and followed Nancy out of the green room.

"Let's check out backstage," Nancy suggested, leading the way up the brick corridor. "That's where Jackie spent most of her time at the theater. If she was going to leave any clues, she'd leave them there."

Entering the scenery storage area, Nancy noticed an open box of tools on the floor: hammers, wrenches, and crowbars. She paused to think for a moment. Rosa had been struck with a blunt instrument. How simple it would have been for Jackie to obtain such a thing. . . .

Nancy knelt by the toolbox. Covering her hand with her sweatshirt sleeve to avoid leaving new fingerprints, she shifted the tools around. "Let's see if any of these tools has blood on it."

"Wouldn't Jackie have enough sense to clean a bloody tool before returning it to the box?" Bess pointed out. "You don't have to be a professional criminal to think of that."

"All the same," Nancy said, "we should tell Zhang about this toolbox. The police forensics lab might find something we can't see with our naked eyes. Any evidence would help at this point." She sat back on her heels."Should we keep on looking?"

Borrowing a flashlight from the toolbox, the girls began to hunt around the darker corners of the storeroom. "Maybe we'll find a bloody tool stashed somewhere," Nancy said.

The flashlight beam reflected off something metallic underneath some lumber scraps. Nancy quickly uncovered the object, only to find that it was a tin of paint solvent. Noticing its cap was half unscrewed, Nancy went to tighten it. A pungent aroma rose from the open spout.

Nancy sniffed and wrinkled her nose. "Shine that beam on the label, George," she said. She pored over the list of chemical ingredients. "This contains formalin—a type of formaldehyde! Maybe the stuff in Marta's atomizer came from here."

Then she frowned. "Trouble is, Greta washed the atomizer out last night. We can't match the substances."

"But someone's prints might be on the can," George said. "Zhang should check this, too."

Just then the rumble of a huge ovation broke out from the stage above them. Bess looked up toward the sound. "Marta's big aria, 'Vissi d'arte,'" she said. "Act Two is almost over."

Nancy looked around anxiously. "We still have to investigate the prop room. But any minute now, the stage crew will be swarming all over this place. We'd better lie low for a while."

The girls slipped into the prop room, just to the side of the main scenery storeroom. Wooden shelves lining the walls were piled high with a jumble of items—everything from baskets of plastic flowers for *Figaro* to stacks of rifles for the third act of *Tosca.* Nancy and her friends huddled down behind a large trunk in the corner.

Curious, George reached out to touch the guns. "Wow, these are real," she whispered.

"They need real guns to fire real-sounding shots when Cavaradossi's executed," Bess said.

"Tosca's boyfriend gets executed?" Nancy said. "I've never seen Act Three. I was too busy in Marta's dressing room last night to watch it."

"Yeah, he's sentenced to death," Bess said. She paused as stagehands shouted to each other in the set storeroom. "Tosca tries to save him," Bess went on quietly, "by getting Baron Scarpia to order a fake execution for Cavaradossi. Then she stabs Scarpia."

George stuck our her tongue. "Yuck."

"Little does she know," Bess continued, "that

Scarpia's pardon was a trick. He secretly ordered the firing squad to use real bullets."

Nancy rolled her eyes. "These opera plots are so far-fetched," she whispered.

The girls sat in silence for several minutes as the stage crew changed the sets. Once the stage was set, the crew left. Only then did the girls crawl out from their hiding place and begin to poke around the props.

"Whoa," George whispered, standing by the gun shelf. "Guys, look."

Nancy and Bess hurried over. George pointed to the floor, where a pile of dull lead bullets lay.

Nancy crouched down to examine them. "But these aren't blanks," she said slowly.

The three girls stared at each other. "Looks like someone's planning a truly authentic performance tonight."

16

Into Thin Air

George and Bess stared at Nancy. "Real bullets?" George echoed. "Who would do such a thing?"

Nancy clutched a handful of bullets and began to head for the door. "Donald, for one."

"But Tompkins isn't in the cast," Bess said, hurrying to keep up with Nancy.

"Oh, yes he is—tonight," Nancy said grimly. "He's taking Mark Stephens's place."

"Oh, no!" Bess cried. "And Mark was supposed to play—"

"One of the soldiers in the firing squad," Nancy finished as she ran through the set storeroom. "Let's hurry. We've got to tell Steven to stop the opera!"

"But Donald wouldn't hurt Marta. He's her biggest

fan!" Bess protested. She leaped forward and grabbed Nancy by the arm.

Nancy spun around to face her friend. "Celebrities have been killed before by their biggest fans," she reminded Bess. "Half-crazed adoration can turn sour at any moment."

Bess's blue eyes flashed. "But the third act has already begun. I don't think Steven would agree to bring down the curtain now." She swallowed. "Look at it from his point of view. So far his productions have been disrupted every single night of this River Heights run. The board of directors is going crazy. He could lose his job over this."

"If Marta is killed onstage, he will most certainly lose his job," Nancy replied. "He won't want to risk the life of his star. He wouldn't risk anybody's life for a mere show."

"Wait, Nancy. There is another way to stop this from happening," George spoke up. Nancy turned to face her; she was happy to hear an alternate solution.

"If Steven stops the show right now," George pointed out, "our culprit will keep on harassing Marta. But if we let the show go on, we could catch him—or her—red-handed. And that would finally put a stop to all this."

Nancy rapidly considered George's plan. "You're

right," she agreed. "But then I've got to make sure things don't go too far. And the only way to do that is—"

She broke off and ran toward the stairs.

With the third act in progress, Lauren wasn't in the wardrobe room to ask why Nancy was in such a hurry to get her nun costume off the rack. The roomy black habit slid on easily over her jeans and sweatshirt. "Thank goodness this didn't happen during *Aida,*" Nancy thought wryly. "I would never have gotten into that skimpy white shift this fast."

Nancy dashed up the hallway and swung through the passage leading onstage. She stopped for a moment in the darkened wings and stared at the people onstage. Where was Marta?

The scenery represented the courtyard of a grim, stone fortress. The floor of the stage was steeply raked toward a knee-high wall at the top. A painted backdrop beyond it represented the fresh blue sky of an Italian morning.

Maybe Marta hadn't made her entrance yet, Nancy considered. Unfamiliar with this part of the opera, she swivelled around, looking for someone to ask.

A motion behind the backdrop caught her eye.

Some sixth sense made Nancy's skin prickle. She stepped around the side pieces of scenery, which were painted like rugged stone columns.

At the back of the stage, the raised acting surface was nearly fifteen feet higher than the real stage floor. A gap of two or three feet formed a sort of narrow canyon between the papier-mâché wall at the top and the sky backdrop. A stack of lumpy mattresses covered the floor at the bottom of the gap.

And there, perched on the mattresses and ready to run, was Jackie Ahern.

Nancy hurtled toward her. Jackie's lithe, boyish body darted across the mattresses and jumped down the other side.

There was no room to squeeze around the mattresses, wedged as they were between the backdrop and the steel risers supporting the raked stage. Fighting her long skirt, Nancy tried to scramble through the risers—but it was tricky. Low struts kept tripping her while higher ones banged her head. Finally she worked her way past the mattresses and ran to the far side of the stage. She looked left, and then right.

No sign of Jackie.

Just then Nancy looked up. There was Jackie, leaning over the railing of the steel catwalk overhead.

Nancy glanced at the spiral staircase that led to the catwalk. She knew if she went up, Jackie would simply run down the stairs on the other side. And

Jackie had a lot more practice than she did navigating the rickety structure.

Nancy swung up the first few stairs, taking them two at a time, despite her heavy skirt. As she'd expected, Jackie skittered off in the other direction. In response, Nancy changed course, vaulting as quietly as she could over the handrail and landing on the stage floor. She ducked into the narrow space behind the backdrop and ran across the stage. Maybe Jackie wouldn't notice Nancy had switched from the catwalk route until they were both on solid ground. . . .

The ruse worked. By the time Nancy emerged from behind the backdrop, Jackie had just jumped off the last step of the spiral staircase. Nancy bounded after her. "How did you get inside the theater?" Nancy asked.

Jackie laughed cynically. "Get inside? I never left. I've been sleeping here all along, right inside the pyramid from *Aida.*"

Dodging Nancy's grasp, Jackie jumped onto a pile of wooden pallets. With a catlike agility, she disappeared behind a jumble of Egyptian-looking statues.

At that moment, the music from the orchestra grew very loud. Nancy looked over her shoulder and saw Marta, standing serenely in the wings, fixing her scarlet cloak in preparation for her entrance.

Nancy weighed her choices. Where would the

danger to Marta be greatest: from the live bullets in the guns onstage, or from Jackie, backstage?

Nancy drew a deep breath and made her decision. Reaching up to straighten her white wimple around her face, Nancy sidled onstage.

It took her a minute to get used to standing on the steeply slanted surface. On the far side of the stage, a band of uniformed soldiers lounged by the side wall of the fortress. Nancy searched the faces beneath their low yellow caps, trying to figure out which one was Donald Tompkins.

In her peripheral vision, she saw the orchestra conductor waving wildly, as if to shoo Nancy off the stage. Nancy willed herself not to look his way. She knew as well as he did that the script didn't call for a nun to be onstage at this point in the opera. *But what the audience doesn't know wouldn't bother them,* she figured. And she didn't intend to disturb matters onstage any more than necessary.

Nancy quickly pinpointed Tompkins. He was the skinny one at the back of the stage. She was certain of it when he turned to gaze at Marta. The soldiers weren't supposed to notice Cavaradossi's scarlet-cloaked visitor, but Donald couldn't help but look.

Moving as slowly and as silently as possible, Nancy edged toward the rampart wall at the back of the set. Marta and the tenor playing Cavaradossi had just launched into a beautiful duet. The audience seemed spellbound by it; too spellbound to notice a stray nun, Nancy hoped.

Nearing the papier-mâché wall, Nancy leaned over just enough to be able to see over it. She was checking to see where Jackie was. The strip of floor behind the ramparts was empty. Good.

Now came the tricky part—getting all the way across stage to be within reach of Donald. Nancy thrust her hands up her wide black sleeves, assumed a meditative air, and paced gravely along the rampart wall.

As she reached the opposite side the two lovers finished their duet and the audience exploded into applause. Then Nancy felt an abrupt change in the music. Military-sounding strains signaled that it was time for the soldiers to swing into action.

The firing squad was beginning to grab their rifles and line up. With unusual haste for a nun, Nancy hitched up her skirt and hustled downstage.

If only I could grab Donald's gun! But which one is his? Nancy thought. Half a dozen rifles were propped up against the fake side wall of the fortress. And only one of them held real bullets, she guessed.

Nancy had no choice but to wait for Donald to make his move. She saw him saunter over to the side wall and pick up a gun. She steadied her nerves and tried to visualize what she anticipated Donald would do.

Cavaradossi was being led center stage for his execution. Tosca had scurried to the other wall, stage right. She was pretty far away from the soldiers, Nancy noted. But if Donald was a trained marksman—and for all she knew, he might be—he could still hit Marta from a distance.

The firing squad marched forward in a line. Nancy edged closer to Donald, muscles tense—ready to pounce.

The firing squad raised their rifles. Donald cocked his head along with the others, squinting down the barrel to take aim.

Nancy raised one hand. Donald's gun was still pointed directly toward Cavaradossi, like the others'. But the moment he swung the barrel in Marta's direction, Nancy would knock it aside—

Fire! Several rifles went off with a sharp crack and tiny puffs of smoke.

But Donald didn't even pull his trigger.

As Cavaradossi crumpled to the ground the firing squad lowered their guns and turned away. So did Donald.

Nancy leaned back against the wall. No live bullets had been fired, had they? A quick glance at the fallen tenor showed the rise and fall of his breathing. He might be acting dead, but he was alive and well.

As the soldiers began to file offstage Nancy stiffened. Donald wasn't going with them! Pulling his yellow cap down low, he plunked himself on a bench, his rifle beside him.

Nancy held her breath. At this point in the scene, there shouldn't be a soldier onstage (or a nun either, of course). What was Donald going to do?

Marta was heading for center stage, singing to her dead lover, urging him to wake up. Nancy stared at Donald's hand, still resting lightly on his gun. He could snatch it up and fire at any moment.

Suddenly Baron Scarpia's henchmen burst onto the stage. Tosca, only beginning to realize that Cavaradossi was truly dead, reeled away from them. She staggered upstage, climbing the steep slope, heading for the rampart wall.

It all came to Nancy in a flash. It was the only suitable finale: Tosca was going to fling herself to her death from the prison ramparts.

That was why the mattresses had been stacked there, to break Marta's fall when she jumped.

Only the mattresses weren't there anymore, were they? The floor was clear. Nancy had seen that with her own eyes, only she hadn't realized why they were missing. *Jackie must have moved those mattresses,* Nancy thought.

And any second now, Marta was going to jump.

17

Curtain Call

Nancy gazed anxiously back and forth between the singer and Donald. What to do? If she ran upstage to prevent Marta from jumping off the parapet, Donald might shoot Marta. Nancy cast a pleading glance into the wings. Was there anyone who could restrain Donald while she ran after Marta?

Then, in the dimness of the wings, Nancy saw a blond head. Bess! Nodding vigorously and pointing to Donald, Bess signaled to Nancy that she'd take care of the obsessed fan with the gun.

Nancy was free to follow Marta.

Giving Donald a sudden shove toward the wings, Nancy pivoted and sprinted upstage. She silently apologized to Steven for spoiling another of his productions—and just at the heartbreaking climax!—

then shoved up her sleeves. *I wish I knew this opera better,* she said to herself. *I'll just have to guess when Marta's about to stop singing and jump.*

Marta hit a thrilling high note. Nancy paused within arm's reach of the singer.

Suddenly there was a commotion behind her. A murmur broke from the audience. Nancy turned to see Donald swinging his rifle, knocking Bess aside. Then he dropped the gun and he too ran headlong upstage toward Marta.

Marta stared at the nun and the soldier bearing down on her, but she didn't stop singing. She flung her arms out and finished with Tosca's last cry of defiance. Then she gathered her voluminous skirts and hopped up on top of the rampart wall.

With a mad cry of his own, Donald flung himself at Marta, throwing his arms around her and pulling her back onto the stage. They tumbled down the raked floor and fell into a heap.

"Curtain!" Nancy heard someone yell from backstage. It was probably Doug, the stage manager. The orchestra continued to play, but the velvet curtain tumbled down, hiding the chaos from the audience.

A roar of applause rose from the other side.

"They think that's the way the opera's supposed to end!" cried the actor playing Scarpia's lieutenant. "These small-town cultureless people!"

Shaken, Marta had pushed Donald away and was hauling herself to her feet. "Donald, why did you do that?" she scolded him, blue eyes blazing. "Tosca isn't supposed to be captured. She's supposed to jump!"

"But look, Marta." Donald guided her to the ramparts' edge. Together they peered over. "No mattresses!"

Nancy joined them to gaze down at the ominous empty gap. Far below, she saw George wrestling Jackie to the floor.

Marta turned to Donald and threw her arms around his neck. "My dear, loyal Donald!" She enclosed him in a smothering hug.

Steven came charging up the sloping stage. "Marta, what happened?" Nancy stepped forward and quickly filled him in.

Steven patted Donald's back. "I don't know why you were onstage, Tompkins, but I'm glad you were." He glanced over his shoulder toward the audience. "And now, Marta, I think these folks deserve a curtain call. Can you manage that?"

Marta looked disoriented, but she gamely nodded and marched toward the curtain with Steven. She lined up with Cavaradossi, now on his feet again, and Sean Torrance, who had sung Scarpia in the performance. Holding hands, they proceeded through the part in the curtain. The ovation was overwhelming.

Nancy turned to Donald. "How did you know?"

"Please don't tell Marta," Donald pleaded, taking both Nancy's hands in his. "It all started innocently. I never thought it would go so far!"

"Never thought *what* would go so far?"

Donald hung his head. "Jackie and I met outside the stage door a few weeks ago. We started chatting, as fellow fans do. She said she had a plan to get back at Rosa for insulting Marta. Well, of course the idea appealed to me. Just a few 'mishaps.' That's all they were meant to be."

Nancy processed this as they walked toward the wings. "So you were helping her?"

"At first." Donald nervously fingered his goatee. "Marta often invites me into her dressing room during intermission, so one night a couple weeks ago, when she was changing, I . . . I borrowed a few of Marta's trinkets."

Nancy snapped her fingers. "That *was* you!"

Donald nodded. "I gave them to Jackie, who said she could pin the theft on Rosa. I tried to choose less valuable stuff so Marta wouldn't be upset, but later I found out I'd taken Mario's old presents. I felt terrible! I stole them back from Jackie's hiding place in the pyramid. I was trying to return them, piece by piece."

Now that they had reached the side wings, Nancy paused. "So it was you who left that note saying, 'Butterfly must die'?"

Donald looked stricken. "What? I never heard of such a thing! That must have been Jackie!"

Nancy waved that aside. "What else did you do for Jackie?"

"I slashed Paula Konstance's tires Tuesday morning so Jackie could snip Rosa's corset," Donald admitted. "But after that, I saw things were turning nasty. After Marta was given that bad throat spray, I was upset. I was ashamed to show my face around the theater! I wanted to tell Marta, but . . ." He looked miserable. "I kept chickening out. I knew I'd have to confess my part in the whole sordid matter. I couldn't face that."

"But you could have prevented so many people from being hurt," Nancy told him.

"I know," Donald groaned. "So tonight, I decided to do the next best thing. I would become Marta's onstage bodyguard. I got a costume from Lauren and showed up as a soldier." He struck a military pose. "No one thought to stop me. I even put real bullets in my gun so I could shoot anyone who tried to hurt Marta."

Donald blinked and added lamely, "Of course, I've never shot a gun before. I suppose I would have missed."

He's totally nuts, Nancy thought. But she guessed his loyalty to Marta and desire to protect her would probably get him off the hook. Who would ever press charges against the man who'd just saved Marta Wil-lentz's life?

Nancy gave Donald a stern look. "Did you ever ask why Jackie would do this to her own mother?"

"Her *mother?*" Donald looked shocked. "Marta?"

"Yes—didn't she tell you?"

Donald began to tug frantically on his goatee. "No, never. Marta has no daughter! Everyone knows that."

Then something over Donald's shoulder caught Nancy's attention. Marta was standing right behind him, clutching her curtain call bouquets—and her face drained of color. "That girl—is my *daughter?*"

Nancy felt terrible. Stepping around Donald, she took Marta by the elbow. "I'm sorry you had to find out this way. Sean knew. He was going to tell you."

Marta turned to her left. Sean was standing there. There was still fake blood all over the chest of his black brocade tunic, where Tosca had stabbed the evil Baron Scarpia.

Sean stammered, "I didn't know it was Jackie at first. She was the same girl who showed up in San Francisco."

"She came to San Francisco?" Marta raised her eyebrows.

"Yes, six months ago—the night you sang *Butter-fly* there." Sean faltered. "I spoke to her backstage.

She wanted to force herself on you there, in mid-performance. I wouldn't let her." His voice broke. "I was protecting you!"

Just then the milling backstage crowd parted. Detective Zhang shouldered his way through, pulling Jackie toward the door. Handcuffs glittered on Jackie's wrists.

Nancy saw Marta's face struggle with a host of emotions. She stepped forward to block Jackie's path. A hush fell over the crowd.

Marta faced Jackie, drawing herself up to her full height. Then, suddenly, she seemed to collapse, like a balloon losing its air. "If you're my daughter," she whispered to Jackie, "why would you want to hurt me?"

Jackie's pale gray eyes tightened, turning icy cold. "You rejected me years ago," she spat at Marta. "Why *wouldn't* I want to hurt you?"

"But to go to such lengths!" Steven, at Marta's side, exclaimed.

Jackie's face twisted into a cruel sneer. *Her polite, nervous manner fooled everybody, including me,* thought Nancy. *She's as good an actress as her mother!*

"How hard was it?" Jackie exulted. "Sneaking into the theater was a piece of cake. Sawing the struts off that backdrop in Preston City? Easy. But when I was waiting backstage to push the scenery over on Marta, Jerry Cropper chased me off." Her eyes glinted. "I made sure he paid for that."

Steven rubbed his forehead. "And then you had the gall to apply for his job."

Jackie shrugged. "Why not? I had experience. And once I was in the company, it was even easier to make Marta's life difficult. A little shove to a sandbag, a little paint solvent in the throat spray . . ." Suddenly she lunged at Marta, though Zhang's strong arm held her back. "Trouble was, you kept getting away safely."

"But why go after Rosa, too?" Nancy asked.

Jackie smirked. "I *had* to humiliate her with that dress popping open—after she said all those mean things about my mom."

Nancy frowned. Jackie hated her mom, but she must love her too, in some warped way. Otherwise, why would she care what Rosa said about Marta?

"And the unhinged parapet?" Steven asked.

Jackie glared toward Sean. "That was aimed at you, to pay you back for not letting me talk to my mom in San Francisco."

"But last night—it was you who attacked Rosa, no? You could have killed her," Marta said gravely.

Jackie hung her head sullenly. "I thought it was you in that purple cape." Then she lifted her head, eyes flashing. "I didn't want to kill you; I just wanted an accident to end your career! Then you . . ." She looked away, a sob choking her voice. "Then maybe you'd finally have time for me."

Marta looked troubled. "I just don't understand. You did all this to ruin me—then you expected me to retire and want to spend time with you?"

Jackie raised a tear-stained face to her mother. "I didn't know how else to get through to you! Your music and fame were always in the way. Your circle of protectors." She looked around at Sean, Donald, Greta, Steven, and Nora, who now appeared at the edge of the crowd. "They're your family, not me. I just wanted you to let me in."

Marta trembled and lowered her eyes. "If you had just written a letter or something, don't you think I would have welcomed you? I've spent every day of the last twenty years wondering if I did the right thing by giving you up. Wondering where you were, what you looked like . . ." She looked up, her face crumpled with sorrow. "I rehearsed in my head a thousand different scenes of meeting you. But I never could have dreamed up a bizarre script like this."

Mother and daughter locked tearful gazes. "And now, I can't afford to lose you again," Marta said softly. "It will be hard to build a relationship, with you in jail. But we should try."

Sean put a comforting arm around Marta. He led her in one direction, while Detective Zhang led Jackie in another.

As the crowd broke up, Nancy joined George and Bess. The stage crew had gone back to work, trundling away scenery. *Tosca* was over, and it was time to set the stage for *Aida*.

"Thanks for all your help tonight, guys," Nancy said. "We took a chance, letting the show go on. But it worked."

Bess sighed. "I just wish this mystery had turned out better. I feel so sad for Jackie and Marta."

Nancy slung her arms around her two friends and grinned ruefully as they walked offstage. "Well, what did you expect from this opera—a happy ending?

Test your detective skills with these spine-tingling Aladdin Mysteries!

The Star-Spangled Secret
By K. M. Kimball

Secret of the Red Flame
By K. M. Kimball

Scared Stiff
By Willo Davis Roberts

O'Dwyer & Grady
Starring in Acting Innocent
By Eileen Heyes

Ghosts in the Gallery
By Barbara Brooks Wallace

The York Trilogy By Phyllis Reynolds Naylor

Shadows on the Wall

Faces in the Water

Footprints at the Window

Have you read all of the Alice Books?

❑ THE AGONY OF ALICE
Atheneum Books for Young Readers
0-689-31143-5
Aladdin Paperbacks
0-689-81672-3

❑ ALICE IN RAPTURE, SORT OF
Atheneum Books for Young Readers
0-689-31466-3
Aladdin Paperbacks
0-689-81687-1

❑ RELUCTANTLY ALICE
Atheneum Books for Young Readers
0-689-31681-X

❑ ALL BUT ALICE
Atheneum Books for Young Readers
0-689-31773-5

❑ ALICE IN APRIL
Atheneum Books for Young Readers
0-689-31805-7

❑ ALICE IN-BETWEEN
Atheneum Books for Young Readers
0-689-31890-0

❑ OUTRAGEOUSLY ALICE
Atheneum Books for Young Readers
0-689-80354-0
Aladdin Paperbacks
0-689-80596-9

❑ ALICE IN LACE
Atheneum Books for Young Readers
0-689-80358-3
Aladdin Paperbacks
0-689-80597-7

❑ ALICE THE BRAVE
Atheneum Books for Young Readers
0-689-80095-9
Aladdin Paperbacks
0-689-80598-5

❑ ACHINGLY ALICE
Atheneum Books for Young Readers
0-698-80533-9
Aladdin Paperbacks
0-689-80595-0

❑ ALICE ON THE OUTSIDE
Atheneum Books for Young Readers
0-689-80359-1
Coming from Aladdin Paperbacks
in Fall 2000